The Silver Vessel

Tracey Fuller

Biscuit Publishing

Published by Biscuit Publishing Ltd 2005

ISBN 1-903914-17-5

A catalogue for this book is
available from the British Library

First published in Great Britain by
Biscuit Publishing Ltd, 2005
PO Box 123, Washington,
Newcastle upon Tyne
NE37 2YW

Typeset by Mike Wilson, Bridlington

Cover design by
Stuart Hodgson © [www.creative-insight.net]

Printed and bound in Great Britain by
Jasprint Ltd, Tyne & Wear

Tracey Fuller won the 2003 Biscuit Prize for Short Fiction with her story *The System Was Turned On* which is published in the prizewinners' anthology *The Sensitively Thin Bill of the Shag*. She was also a runner-up for the 2002 Biscuit Prize and had her story *The Shower* published in the anthology *Adrift, From Belize to Havana*.

She has read her work at the prestigious Voice Box at the Royal Festival Hall on the South Bank and at the Middlesex University Literature Festival and has stories published in Middlesex University Press. She gained an MA in Creative Writing at Middlesex University.

Tracey lives in Sussex and enjoys finding time, with her husband, to ride Daisy – their tandem – around the countryside. Their most important job at the moment, however, is looking after their new baby.

Acknowledgements

I would like to thank my family for providing me with my inspiration for *The Silver Vessel*. Without my Granfer's seafaring stories or Ian's family's old photographs there would not be a story. Thanks to Neil for putting me right with my boaty terms. And thanks to The Imperial War Museum, Newhaven Museum and Newhaven Fort. Also thanks to Sue Gee for her guidance. I would also like to thank the Coxswain Ian 'Paddy' Johns and the crew of the Newhaven lifeboat for listening to the lifeboat sections. The time I spent reading to the crew in the lifeboat house was fantastic. I have never seen men of the sea so quiet! I'd also like to thank Ian for his endless patience, support and amazing creative mind. This book is half his.

The Silver Vessel

Tracey Fuller

Prologue

Jason Tempest
August 1974
Sussex Coast

'I'm going to throw a line over.' The boy hurls an imaginary rope over a wooden gate in the lane. 'Put out your fenders, I'm coming alongside.' He flings out a fender, making it fast with a clove hitch and bumps along the side of the fence.

The lane is deserted. Thwump. Up goes the second maroon, the rocket from the lifeboat house on the dock.

'It's all right, I'm already on it,' he whoops, as he shins up the fence. Standing on the top he wavers a little. 'Don't worry, I'll save you,' he shouts to the hydrangeas. 'Do not fear. I'm coming aboard,' he proclaims to the watering can. Instead of jumping down he swings on top of a shaky looking shed.

'I'm taking the wheel, we'll soon have her ship shape,' he hollers to the sky. He steps forward and grasps the wheel midair. His foot slips; the felt covering the shed roof is weak. It rips, the wood cracks and Jason spins from the deck through to the cabin below.

Silence, except for the ticking of a clock. Then a pain wells up in his ankle and he lets out a scream. There's blood and ripped trousers but when the pain dies he is able to appreciate that it is a cut worthy of a lifeboat man.

He is sprawled on top of cardboard boxes and the hand that he flung out to stop his fall is grazed and twisted. There's the smell of sawn wood and the inside of old clocks. He tries to stand and the cut on his ankle starts bleeding again. Jason's heart leaps into his mouth. The shed is so full of junk that the door is jammed shut. He feels a flutter of panic like a frightened insect in the pit of

7

his stomach. Pressing his eye to a crack in the wood as if it were a telescope, he searches the garden for ships and help.

His Grandmother Lillian finishes pegging out a pair of flared jeans on the line next to a striped silk poncho and heads back to the house.

Pulling aside boxes and broken deckchairs, Jason reaches for the door. A lawnmower arm is wedged under the latch. He searches for something solid amongst the billowing bags of softness to hammer away the handle. A stone or rock would do, but all he can reach are clothes and curtains and cracked umbrellas. He tries to stand. Wobbling on the soggy cardboard and saggy bags he reaches for a small paint tin to knock way the lawnmower arm. His hand slips and goes straight through a damp box landing on something hard and ridged and oval. Jason pulls it out. It is dark green and fits snugly into his hand. It's the perfect rock shape he needs to smash away the latch. One swipe and the handle shifts, the door flies open with the weight of the contents and Jason lands on the grass amid the tumble.

He limps inside the house, leaving the ruptured contents of the shed spilt across the garden, clutching his dark green rock.

Jason can't wait for the morning. He wants the bomb disposal men from the army to still be there, curled up asleep on the floor of the living room, ready to leap into action. There's so much stuff around the house there could easily be a Sherman tank under the stairs or an old howitzer hidden in the airing cupboard.

It's barely light when he peers out of his bedroom window. A breeze rumples the bin bags lying on the lawn. Shapes loom in the half-light. He can almost see waves in the ruffles of material and a boat in the boxes, navigating a rough sea.

Jason and his Nana sit in the debris of his adventure,

amongst the guts of the shed, separating the contents into piles:

1 things for the dump

2 things for the Lifeboat

3 things to definitely be kept

4 things to be investigated further as soon as he can get the rest of the junk sorted.

They are now onto this last pile. They haven't unearthed any more hand grenades but Jason has discovered two grubby and dented tankards. The vessels glow dully at him. He wonders if they might be worth cleaning up. He lifts one of the tankards out of the box and holds it up in the sunlight. Lettering runs around the rim underneath a pattern of leaves. He rubs the letters with his finger, spits and shines the spot with a piece of gauzy curtain. The metal begins to shine silver. It winks at him. The letters become clearer, they're old fashioned and curly and he can't decipher any of them.

'Looks like silver.' Jason turns to his Nana.

She takes the vessel tenderly. 'Solid silver.' She brushes a hand to her eye.

'Was it for valour?' Jason had heard the words some-where before and thought they sounded right.

'For valour, or some kind of courage.'

ONE

Alfie LeBurn
15th April 1912
Sussex Coast

A white cloud explodes in the blue sky. Then the fizz from the maroon as it's sent up from the lifeboat house and then the thump that you can feel through the ground and in your lungs. The second thump comes almost immediately, and the seagulls go wild with their yaking and screeching.

We're out from school and rush to the dock to watch the show. The lifeboat men come running towards the puffs of smoke which hang over the water. We throw ourselves into the hedge as the men fly past on bicycles, dust flying as they skid down Marine Road. They fling the cycles into the grass and run. Behind them wives, some with faces like thunder, muttering about boats always needing rescuing when the dinner's about to be put on the table. Children follow. A baby gathered up and perched on the hip of an eight-year-old girl, its white blanket trailing in the earth after her. Through the long grass they run, short cutting across the field. Children on scooters and two boys on a packing crate go-cart follow, whooping.

Up the wooden steps two or three at a time the crew leap, we stand well back. At the top, with the door open, stands my Father, Jerry, handing out sou'westers and blocky cork lifejackets.

Then, screaming down the road comes Wilfred Kay the lifeboat mechanic in his car Ophelia. The Coxswain, Sam Tempest, is by his side as always. Sam's on the running board, door open, children cheering, Wilf driving, brow furrowed with concentration. Sam is out, he lets the door flap and leaps up the steps. Wilf heaves the handbrake on and slams the doors, leaving the car skewed across the road.

We rush round the front of the lifeboat hut and peer in at the open doors. The boat hovers, towering above, suspended on a white rocker. In gold letters the words *Lady Lucille Maythorpe* shine against the blue paint. The men clamber aboard and Dad takes a hammer. With one swipe he knocks out the holding pin.

Slide, swish, shout. The tide is out and there a drop. The *Lucy May* drops off the end of the slipway, stern first. But she's unsinkable our *Lucy May*. The men, busy rigging, dive uphill to the front of the boat away from the stern as she hits the water. A great wave washes over the deck and she disappears. We get as close as possible to get a drenching from the wash. The men turn their back on it bracing themselves for the bump as she rolls up and we clap and yell as the stern appears again out of the surf, soaking.

Now Jacky Prentice from the butcher's is here, his bicycle flying away from him at right angles. He charges down the quay. Dad is throwing a sou'wester at him. We climb onto the rail guarding the slipway.

Go on Jacky.

People are holding their breath. Sam is on the rail of the boat; he's holding out his hand and shaking his head at the same time, willing Jacky to jump and not to jump.

Go on Jacky.

The *Lucy May* surges and dips in the waves. People line Marine Road. The fishermen smoking the mackerel blink, red-eyed from the smokehouse. Women wipe their slick gutting knives on their aprons and stand up from their spot on the quay. They are flushed with work and the reflection of the sun on stone.

Go Jacky go.

The lifeboat gets as close as it can to the harbour wall. Jacky leaps. It seems as if he is suspended in the air like a character from a comic strip, his sou'wester held high in

11

an arc over his head, Sam grabs his arm and they collapse on the deck. We scream and shout and stamp, the smokehouse and icehouse and gutting shed and all. We re-enact the leap all the way home.

Wilfred Kay
15th April 1912
Sussex Coast

I can't believe he made that jump. Mad Jacky, always late, buttons done up wrong, strong as they come. Training to be a navigator and can't find his way out of a paper bag. The crowds that gathered. You wouldn't think there were so many people on the dock. And there was Sam with his helping hand as ever. Unsinkable.

'Get your life jacket on Jacky, it's blowing up an eight out there. Is anyone pulling in fenders?'

'Keep your hair on Sam, we can see the casualty with our own bloody eyes, we'll be there in no time,' and we knuckle down to it, the waves roughing us up a bit as we head out of the harbour. I'm on the engine praying, as always, that she'll keep us going. Her heat making me sweat under my jacket and life vest. I'll be glad of the biting wind when we're out there and out of this inferno.

It takes fifteen Hail Marys to get out of the harbour, it doesn't seem to matter what the weather is like, maybe I slow down deliberately when the sea is rough. I could close my eyes and still know where we are by the number I've muttered under my breath. Once we're out and past the lighthouse we can see the casualty clearly. She's floundering on the sandbank we call The Ship Swallower, her sails flapping like a demented albatross. It takes us a while to get a line on board. Jacky having a go to make up for his idiocy earlier. His throw is superb. Sam is wrestling with the tiller trying to focus on something on the horizon to keep her straight but the rise and fall of the boat is throwing him out. I'm battling with the engine, singing to her, caressing her. 'Come on Lucy, run sweet for me, there's a girl.' Sometimes I feel a fool but I know they don't care what I do just as long as I keep the damn thing going. None of us fancies rowing in this. Then an almighty wave boils up from the depths of hell and crashes onto the deck and sends Jacky spinning over the side.

'Man overboard.' Ted, our Navigator, is on it, pointing at the spot where Jacky has gone over. Even in the swell of the sea he keeps his finger on the place in the churning waves. Sam spins the nose upwind and we are travelling away from where Jacky went in. This is the bit every man who goes overboard dreads, when the boat moves away to turn around before returning.

'Don't worry Jack, we'll be back, you know the drill mate,' Ted shouts to the place in the waves where he saw Jacky go down.

'Come on lads we can do this. Focus.' Sam yells.

Before I know it I've caught Sam's eye and I'm off the engine and ready to take over. A smudge of yellow in the grey water, that's all and Sam has done it, he's over the side, Ted pointing and shouting directions. Sam has done the one thing he shouldn't but I knew from the moment the wave hit that he would jump. He should never leave his boat and crew, he should never jump into the water, and the procedure we've rehearsed Sunday after Sunday is destroyed by that single leap.

I battle with the helm. A wave hits and jabs the tiller sharp back into my stomach. For all his size Sam is not as strong as me and I keep that boat fixed on the point where he went in. There's no colour in the water. It's just grey and white and I'm praying now to St. Anthony to bring back the things that are lost. I promise that next time I can't find where I've left my Woodbines I will never bother him again if he will just find Sam and Jacky and bring them back from the deep. I even promise to learn to swim in some rash moment of terror. But I know that when we get back I will conveniently forget this one. If you need to swim you're a bad sailor.

13

We seem to be suspended in a swaying swell of motion. I'm concentrating so hard that I feel the blood pumping in my ears and I'm getting cramp in my forearm from the strain of the helm. Even the crew of the boat we are here to rescue are hanging onto the guard rail, holding their breath. Then a yellow arm and a head and two heads burst from the water heaving, and the lifebelt is thrown over and I hurriedly cross myself and coax The *Lucy May* round so we can pick them up. The crew of the stricken boat cheer but all I can think of is holding her steady and I'm talking to The *Lucy May*, willing her to make this easy for us and she does, like an angel she stays where I put her and her engine keeps turning over. She dips down in the trough of a wave just as Sam and Jacky are lifted high above us, they seem to dangle like marionettes for a moment until the wave turns and they are spat out of the wall of water and hauled vomiting and retching onto the deck.

Sam rolls over, looks up at me and smiles.

'Lucky bastard,' I mutter, pulling my eyes away. He grins again and I catch him out of the corner of my eye as he gets shakily to his feet, leans over the side and spits. Then he strides back across the boat

'Give me the tiller Wilf. Are you after my job?' And he takes the helm once more. I think he even winks as he says it. He is dripping but there is not even the hint of a shiver.

Ted and Stan wrap Jacky in blankets and he sits, head in hands, shaking slightly.

'Cut that line Stormy, and get another over.' Sam yells and we are back at the rescue.

After that we seem to do everything like clockwork. I'm back on the engine. Every now and then when I catch Sam's eye I say a quick prayer of thanks under my breath so he can't see.

We tow the boat in. The light is fading and the crowds are gone. There is no one to see our victorious return. The boat trails behind us, its sails piled on the deck, like a whipped pup on a lead.

TWO

Wilfred Kay
16th April 1912
Sussex Coast

It's one of those mornings when the tide is in and the mud in the river is covered with water. When I'm glad to be alive and I'm full of the rescue from the day before, when I've now forgotten my fear at almost losing Sam and his thoughtless bravery or stupidity or whatever I called it yesterday. Today, it is one of those rescues to go down in our personal histories, to be recounted and embellished with the boys in The Naval Volunteer. Sam's foolishness is already heroic, his thoughtlessness is brave and I can barely remember the freezing sweat of fear when he leapt overboard.

I'm trying not to think about the passengers and crew from that other ship who were waving and drowning and freezing in another sea while we were out there. Somehow instead of dwelling on the picture in my head, it makes me even gladder to be alive, even more thankful.

So it is a day for feeling smug and pleased with myself. Not a day to dwell on why we do it; why we go out there in the first place week after week. Strangely people don't seem to ask me why I do it. Good job really because I don't suppose I could answer them. None of the boys could. We just do it. Some do it because their fathers were lifeboat men and their fathers before them and it's just expected. It's nothing to do with heroism or bravery or courage or any of that piffle. Not for me anyway, not for most of them come to that. Maybe for Sam it is, but he's the exception. It has more to do with the nights afterwards in the bar. The way people look at you in the street, knowingly, respectfully as some pillar of the community, I find that part a bit much. When they look at us with a certain amount of awe. But Sam loves it. It's all a load of hogwash. They should see us out there sometimes, hanging on by tooth and nail and being buffeted and thrown about. It's hardly dignified not being able to walk a straight line down The *Lucy May*'s deck or throwing up over the side. Barking at each other, swearing with the terror of it or sick with the boredom of it. But I think Sam enjoys the adulation, for him it makes up for this other stuff, the things we don't talk about. There's the excitement of course, when the maroon goes off and you don't know what you're facing. You have the perfect excuse to leave the ordinary and the everyday to others. I can leave the smoke and steam and noise of the railway for the clean water and a certain kind of peace. For Sam he leaves his solitary boat building for the comradeship of the crew.

Then there's the fact that we do it because it is there, because it needs doing. For me, I couldn't trust someone else to do it. Maybe it's because of the sea itself. The great thrashing expanse of it and knowing that out there is a frail piece of humanity smashing around in the waves that would like another chance and if we can give them that chance then we have to. We just have to.

I often wonder what goes through the minds of those aboard when they see us crashing through the waves. There's something moving about the way our lifeboat will wait with a stricken vessel. Half the time they must wonder what the hell such an insignificant boat can do for them, especially if I've failed with the engine and we're rowing. It must be worse still for a floundering ship. We are nothing in comparison and sometimes we can do little but watch and wait with them until the weather changes, the sea state alters, courage fills us, our prayers are answered. We wait. We will not leave them and I hope we are a comfort. We have our own Gethsemanes out there. If we ever have to leave a stricken vessel, something twists in my stomach as their hope disappears. That's all we are, hope.

After the blow of yesterday the wind has dropped. I take Ophelia, early, up onto the cliffs to catch the best of the sunrise. She's only a car but she feels like more than that to me. The sisters at the convent wanted some work done, a bit of gardening and some work on their stove, nothing much and I had some time. That's when I found her, in an old shed with the work tools. What a sight, rusted and battered. They didn't know what to do with her. They named her, not me, but like a boat you can't change a name. She's looking pretty good now though, her engine goes like a dream.

We slip through the streets scattering cats pawing a scull outside the fish market. The bakery has its door flung open; steam from the ovens beads the window panes. Ophelia, open topped, makes me feel alive just to be inside her and rushing through the air. She cradles me. Sometimes at night, I curl up in the passenger seat, throw a coat over me, slip back against the leather and gaze up at the stars.

The headland is hazy and I climb out of the car and watch until the mist is burnt off by the strengthening sun. I look at the point where yesterday we battled with the swell. Today it is flat calm and deceptively still. In the town beyond, an arm pushes into the sea. A spit of metal, wood and glass that is the pier is strung with lights from turret to cupola. From here it is a dreamlike thing, shadowy and frail, a skeleton of struts picking its way through the waves. And on the end, where the soft edge nudges its way into the sea, I see her in my mind, stretching. She holds her arms wide to the waves, up on her toes, her arms taut against the rail, using it like a ballet bar. She smoothes her hair into a knot and releases it to be flicked by the wind. I can't really see her of course and have never seen this part of her, the preparation, the mental effort, the getting dressed in her slick bathing suit, peeling off the trousers, so outrageous on a woman. I imagine her shape in those trousers, her legs sharply defined, the curve of her bottom, the hug of her hips, the crease between her thighs. She is honey splashed by the sun and her chestnut hair is protected by a hat like an unopened tulip.

I've been getting off work early and joining the crowd, usually for her last show.

Stella Maris, Star of the Sea.

There's gossip about her of course. There is always gossip about women like that, ones who aren't afraid to stand out from a crowd, to use their bodies. She needs some courage, to put up with that, that's for sure. They all think it scandalous but people still flock to see her. I hear them afterwards, in the tea rooms and in the queue for the coconut shy, marvelling at her and shunning her at the same time.

Stella Maris,
Star of the Sea,
Diving Belle.

I think she may have started to notice me. She seems to catch my eye when she is doing her talk before she climbs onto the diving ledge. And that's the other thing people don't like: a one woman show. There's no man to introduce her or do the talky bits, to sensationalise her feats. She is not just a magician's prop or the simpering little woman waiting to fly from the edge at his command. She does it all herself. She doesn't seem to need a man. I think people find that a threat. It exhilarates me.

Stella Maris
31st May 1912
Sussex Coast

He's here again, hovering near the back with a half smile on his thin lips. Dark eyes sparkling and wicked, so wicked I need to turn away and concentrate on the rest of the crowd. He doesn't take his eyes off me and if I dare to catch them it feels as if he is undressing me and reaching into my soul at the same time. I try not to look at him too much, I need to concentrate. He's been coming here almost every day now and I'm beginning to look out for him although I hardly dare admit it to myself. The last few days I've been getting those stupid sick feelings about half an hour before the show, wondering if he will come. If he doesn't show up it's better because I'm not then in danger of losing my footing or forgetting my lines but if he doesn't come . . .

Sometimes when he smiles at me I can't speak, can't breathe even. No man has done that to me before. He makes me nervous but I try to brazen it out. I don't think he noticed me stumble over my words and feet last night.

He was here yesterday and I felt naked. It was the first time that I have stood in my bathing suit in front of a crowd and felt totally naked. I know people are shocked by a woman taking off her clothes but I can hardly dive wearing a dress now can I? It wouldn't be safe or elegant. Anyway I like the excitement of it, the fact that I am so undressed and uninhibited when they are trussed up like legs of lamb in the burning sun. I see the men running their fingers around the edge of their collars and I wonder if it is the heat of the day or seeing a woman so bare in a public place. I notice their wives looking sideways at their men and I smile and feel powerful. I manage to make them all quake and squeal and get hot under the collar. Except him. He just stands there, weight on one hip, half smiling. His dark hair and eyes and hollowed out cheeks. By the time I come back up the ladder and take my bows and the crowds start to disperse he turns and walks away with a faint swagger in his slim hips. The wind gusts and I am left shivering, the pier planks pooled in water about my feet.

Wilfred Kay
1st June 1912
Sussex Coast

'What time do you get off?' I lean against the wall of the workshop and pat my pockets for a packet of Woodbines. If I light up in here, with all the wood shavings and dust, Sam will be furious. It would be madness to let a spark catch but I wonder if I should chance my luck anyway. Sam smoothes his hand over the plank he is planing, feeling for the irregularities in the wood. His fingers find a rise and he leans once again against the plane, one hand forward as a guide, one hand behind steadying. He pushes as if it's a sledge runner against packed snow, stroking firmly.

'Why, what have you in mind?' Sam eyes me leaning against the doorjamb neither in nor out of the workshop. I hover on the edge, hands shoved deep into my pockets, my eyes flicking around the wood and machinery. I'm dying to light up and he knows it.

'Go outside to smoke,' Sam says, just as I decide to stuff it all and reach for my cigarettes. I grin at him, caught out, and move a couple of yards away from the entrance to the workshop. Lighting up I stand with the cigarette behind my back. I take a quick puff when Sam bends his head to shave the piece of wood which is to become a bargeboard.

'So what are we doing then?' Sam smoothes the curls from the plane; the light catches them as they fall. They sink through the sun falling across the workshop, honey soft ringlets, and I can see her hair falling across her shoulders. Once when I arrived early for the show I caught her unpinning her hair, not yet wet from being plunged into water.

'I just thought we could go for a drink. There's a show on the pier you might enjoy.' I rush the last bit and look away down the slipway as if I don't care if we go or not.

'*I* might enjoy?' Sam stops smoothing the wood for a moment. 'I thought you didn't like the pier. If I remember rightly, it's an obscene piece of gaudy tat and you wouldn't be seen dead there.'

'Rubbish, I love the pier.' I'm smiling now.

'You're contrary.' Finishing the planing Sam picks up his tools and places them in their racks. His hand touches the broom but I must look too agitated.

'So what's so great about this show?'

'There's a woman,'

'There's always a woman.'

'Not like this one.'

Sam has his coat now and he's checking everything is in its place. He makes a note for the morning in the dust on the metal table and locks up.

'Her name is Stella.'

'So what's she like this Stella?'

'Star of the Sea.'

'What?' We are walking now and my pace has quickened towards Ophelia.

'You'll see. She has a diving show.' I crank up the engine, 'It's my night Sam, can feel it.' I hop over the door of the car and slide in.

'Do we have to take the car?' Sam throws his jacket in the back anyway. It's good job I know he's joking.

'You might not like her but just think what gives us, independence, the open road, freedom.' I release the brake, Ophelia takes off with a skid and Sam grips the seat, his knuckles white.

THREE

Stella Maris
1st June 1912
Sussex Coast

I stand in front of the crowd, telling them stories of how I came to be able to fly through the air. The same old patter making the children gasp. I flirt outrageously with the young men, flattering the older ones with a flash of my eyes, making the women catch the edge of their companions' sleeves nervously, as if I have a net and am snaring exotic butterflies. Not that there is anything exotic about this crowd. Ladies in safe dresses neatly just on the ankle, men in cloth caps or hats, suited even on this blue day, never willing to take a risk, undo a button or, God forbid, take off a tie. But I widen my eyes and make them all feel special, each one. I catch each person's eye even if just for a moment and lead them with me, making them feel is if they are the only person standing there on the lip of the pier with me and me alone.

I am a magician. I can make everyone else disappear. Even the women loosen their hold on their husband's arms and come with me as I catch them in a web of stories. And just as the enchantment is complete I remove my silk robe. This alone, removing my gown, is enough to make some blush and shudder in anticipation. The children are so captivated they do not nudge or giggle, the men are agog, even the women cannot take their eyes off me. It's been a hot day but it isn't just the heat that is making the men sweat.

Then I see him slipping in at the back of the audience, late for this show, early no doubt for the next and I falter with the string of my gown and I nearly lose them. I throw out my threads again and weave them quickly around my audience; their attention only flickers for a moment.

His hat is pulled down over his eyes and I can only just make them out, a flickering smile passing like a cloud across his mouth. This time he has brought a friend, square shouldered, fair haired, uncomfortable in this setting. He and his friend are newly entered, the worst kind, they are not yet captured and their eyes wander from me to the rest of the audience wondering what this is all about, still agitated with the newness of arrival. His friend looks harassed, as if he has been rushed here or pressured into coming to see this creature. I manage to pull the cord of my robe and let it fall open. I have recaptured my audience. My man has pushed his hat back slightly and raised his eyebrow or perhaps I wish he had. One eye slowly, lazily lowered.

I always pull someone out of the crowd to give me some cover while I am midair, mid-sea and climbing back to the throng. I have never picked out this man at the back although I have wanted to. It would be too close, too intimate somehow, but I can call on his companion. His friend turns, as they do so often, to see if there is some mistake. Surely there is someone far wittier, cleverer, more handsome standing behind them that I require. I wade through the crowd and pull him by the hand, my eyes not on him but on the man who confuses me with his looks and his frequency.

I whisper to the man I have chosen; his name, he says, is Sam. I see his friend look amused, rather than angry or jealous, as if we are sharing in the joke, as if he knew I could not choose him, as if choosing his friend is private enough.

I tell Sam to make up some things to keep the audience wondering if I will come up or not, that last time I did this I nearly drowned, that I was down for five minutes. All this at a whisper while I walk round him, posturing and posing, all part of the act. A sudden squall stirs them up and ravages the women's skirts and sends them swirling. It grabs the hats of the men and swings candyfloss stickily into faces. A woman bends to untangle the mess from her

23

daughter's flying hair. A hat is tugged and torn and rolls away across the planks. Quickly I climb onto the diving platform. I usually start low down at their level and do a few ordinary swallow dives but he has seen those dives before and today I want to impress. Today they will not be enough.

I stand on the platform, heels raised. I walk to the end and fake mock concern at how far down the gnashing waves are. I pirouette. Sam is laughing now, in full swing, pretending it is terribly dangerous, how will I ever survive. I turn and scan the crowd but my man has gone. I turn again a couple of times and search the lines of upturned faces. Sam is looking at me, slightly perturbed, he is expecting me to have done something by now. The crowd shivers like a pack of cards between a magician's fingers. They shuffle and splay out. He is not here. I have chosen his friend over him and he has left in disgust after all. I thought he would be more constant than that. I turn once more and scan the people on the pier, the queue for candyfloss, the children lingering at the carousel, but the crowd is waiting. Sam is faltering. I jump lightly, one foot raised and pointed, swinging my arms for lift. The crowd holds its breath. Between my foot and the diving board they will be able to see the loop of the shore.

A sudden gust of wind blows up from a hovering dark cloud. I leap again. This is to be a defiant dive, a splendid, masculine, strong dive just in case he is still somewhere watching. The gust takes the string of lights which lace the edge of the pier and sets them flying like a necklace flung by a jealous lover. And then I am hit by a bead from the chain, cast-iron and lethal and I spin. My head, already gashed, catches the edge of the dive board and I am out.

Apparently I lose consciousness but I remember it all perfectly. I am plummeting into the blue grey depths too near the pier legs amid the swirling eddies. I am tangled in the crisscross metalwork, barnacled and sharp.

My hair floats about my head like seaweed. I can see

24

him, the man with the smoky eyes and lazy smile. He did not leave after I chose Sam, he came down here into the watery depths to meet me. I reach out to him and he scoops me gently into his arms and lifts me, medusa headed towards the sun which streams through the water like light through church windows.

I am lifted through the shadow of the pier girders and laid on the boards, warm with the heat of the end of the day. I am huddled in a jacket. I come round vomiting water and salt and all manner of detritus, over the boards and my rescuer. He wipes the water from my face and blood from my hair line and cradles me. I look up and see that it is not the man I thought. It is Sam who is holding me, stroking me, his rough hands sandpapering my cheek, making me realise I am alive.

Wilfred Kay
1st June 1912
Sussex Coast

We arrived at the pier early with Sam agitated because I had driven too fast and stopped and started and he was thrown around in his seat. It's only because he isn't used to the car, he loves it and hates it at the same time. He enjoys the feel of the air in his face alright but he hates the speed of it even though he handles speed at sea. I tell him this is just the beginning, that cars will travel at 40mph before long but he doesn't believe they could go much faster than the 20mph that we did today.

We rushed into the back of the crowd, too late for this show and too early for the next, past the posters proclaiming:

Stella Maris, Star of the Sea
Diving Belle
Enchanted Diving Show
3 shows daily 2pm, 4pm and 6pm
Adults one shilling, Children sixpence

I wanted to pull Sam back and get him to see a full show from the beginning but of course as soon as he sees her he is beguiled. So we stay and we watch. I lean against one of the pillars of the pier. I fold my arms, pull down my hat, wonder if I look nonchalant and interesting enough. She has the crowd hovering in the soft crease of her palm, the children wide eyed. I'm more interested in the reaction of the other men. I stand and watch them rather than her. They look as if there is no-one here but her, they are curious about her. They cannot imagine a more wonderful woman. Of course, they do not compare her to their wives: she is in a different category altogether. Their wives would not stand half naked in a public place for a start. They would not have the ability to weave tales, to hold an audience. They would not let their hair go from a clip and let it fall about their shoulders or shake their curls suggestively and they would not flash their eyes, letting them rest on every person individually. Their wives would not be so brazen, so intimate with people they did not know, so lavish with their attentions.

I know what they are thinking because I have thought it all too. They can't fool me with, 'we only come here because the children like the stories.' Men are all the same, they're wondering what it would be like to take off that bathing suit, to peel the straps off the shoulders, pulling it down to her pubic bone and letting it wait there while they drink her in. Watching with delight as her breasts are set free, the nipples, hard, ruffled by the breeze. They are curious about what making love to her would be like, they assume she is far more experienced than their wives, that she would be willing to try the things they only dare dream about. They wonder longingly whether they could mean anything to her, whether they could be the one she would want. Whether she would notice them, what delights she might hold for them. They are curious about how she would sound, what soft noises she would make for them alone, how fast her breathing would be, how heavy, how persistent. They are thinking of what pleasures she could give to them, new pleasures their wives would not dream of offering.

I have dreamt all these things lazily when I am watching her, avidly in the night and I smile at these poor wretches, each one longing for a moment with her. No wonder their women are shocked, horrified, yet in awe and strangely drawn to her.

I wanted something from Sam tonight, something like approval but now I am concerned that even Sam, with his daring and outrageous bravery, may think she is too much of a risk, that I could not, and should not, even try. And how to try? How would you make a move on such a woman? I catch her eye for a second and smile but I want to do something more tangible. I wink and, yes, she's blushing and tugging at the cord of her robe. Her patter falters slightly and I know in that instant that she does feel something for me beyond the other men she sees.

It never enters my head that she might have a husband or even a fiancé although she does not wear a wedding band, I've checked that much. A woman this voluptuous must surely have ensnared a man.

Now she is swimming through the crowd and I wonder what it would be like falling through the water with her in my arms, slippery against my body, her pelvis against my chest, my ribs next to the curve of her waist, my head at her breasts. I would be safe in the sea with her at my side: no thrashing or flapping; she would simply sink with me, plunge and then raise me up, we would curl around each other as we break through the filmy water.

She has her eyes on me. She does not take them from me. She is going to choose me to do her little right hand man puppetry. If that's what she wants I'll do it but it feels too exposed. If she pulls me out the whole audience will know, we won't be able to take our eyes off each other. How will she be able to dive without taking me with her? Then, when she is very close and I can breathe her in, it is as if she has sensed me and she takes Sam's hand instead

27

of mine and leads him back through the crowd. She leads him by putting his hand on her arm; she goes in front through the people holding his hand firmly and looks back over her shoulder at me.

I have to do something, make a gesture, something more than a wink. I have to show her that I am the one who should be chosen, not for the show, but for her. I turn, before she has finished whispering to Sam, because I cannot bear the thought of her parted lips that close to my best friend.

I dodge a carriage on the road beyond the pier and run the gauntlet of a blast of horns as I dash across. The wind rushes in from the sea and tears at me, the sky glowers and a kite which, a few moments earlier, had been dancing in the breeze is turned into a demon, a scudding arrow sent back towards its owner. At the flower stall opposite the pier the blooms are caught in the squall, their petals roughly ripped. And then the wind dies. When she emerges glistening and silky at the end of the show I will give her the bouquet.

The flowers are bewildering and I know nothing about what a woman would desire. How can a flower say everything I want? How can it represent her intellect and mystery as well as being erotic? There are dewy heavy roses, some lilies, too funereal, hollyhocks and marguerite daisies, too innocent. I want to shower her with blossom, pull the petals from heads and sprinkle them over her wet body. I harden at the thought and turn to watch a newspaper flutter across the pavement, the shine of a chromed radiator on a parked car, the red and blue kite whipping through the lemon sun. The feeling subsides and a woman is looking at me, waiting for my order.

'Something for your lady?' she says, pulling stems from buckets and holding them dripping for me to see.

'I want something sharp and soft.' What am I saying? What on earth does that mean? I bet the flower seller has never had a request like that yet I know exactly what I mean and so will Stella. I want something sharply erotic and something soft and sensual as well.

The flower seller blinks and I push my hands into my pockets and think I should just grab a handful of lilies and be done with it. She picks tall blue-grey thistles that have only been used to support heavier bending stems, and vulva-red, gaping snapdragons and yes, she has gone for the roses, top-of-the-milk white with waxy cream centres, heady with scent.

She is wrapping and tying them before I can say yes or no but of course I will say yes. They are perfect and cost more than I thought flowers could, even though the thistles are free because she thinks Stella will throw them out as weeds. I gather them to me. The paper is drenched from the stems. They drip onto my jacket and I turn and dodge the cars once again, heading back to the glinting pier.

The light is starting to fade. A dog, wet through from the sea, stands against the railings shivering. A mass of starlings loop around the helter-skelter. They fold into themselves as more are added to their number. For a few seconds I am mesmerised by how very ordinary birds can transform into a thing of huge beauty and spectacle when gathered together and I wonder if that is what we do for each other.

I rush to her, hoping the flowers will please, wondering whether she will light up slowly from the corners of her mouth, light filling her face, her cheeks, her eyes. I pass the 'A' frame announcing Stella's show and see the crowd has pressed in tightly on itself, packed and murmuring, and the spiky sensations that were gathering in the pit of my stomach and tops of my thighs turn to something more hollow and deadened.

Pushing through the throng I see Sam crouching. Stella is nestled in his sodden jacket in a pool of water, shivering, retching. He is soaked to the skin, they are both shaking, they cannot take their eyes off one another. I see him wipe the blood that threatens to run in tributaries into her eyes and he bends as if to kiss her mouth. Her back arches towards him and I look away. The flowers spill onto the wet boards. Above the pier the starlings swirl. A bolt from the shore shoots into the swirling mass and takes one out. The peregrine tumbles to the beach with its prey, neck broken. Starlings scatter like a blizzard of black snow.

FOUR

Wilfred Kay
2nd June 1912
Sussex Coast

Much later during the madness of war I will recall Sam
and Stella tumbling as one into the car. I will remember it
daily. How like an Indian goddess, arms and legs sprung
from one body, they fell into the backseat. I will remember
being angry at them for bringing soaking seawater into
Ophelia and wetting her leather. I will remember being
agitated that they presumed I would drive them home,
furious that I was not asked to drive Stella to her own
home – wherever home might be for such a creature –
mad that Sam simply assumed that I would take them to
his house. I will not remember that she looked at the back
of my head and glanced at me in the rear view mirror
because I was busy not looking at her huddled in Sam's
arms on the backseat. I just drove too fast and swung
Ophelia around corners making them slide across the
leather and slam into each other.

Sam carried her from the backseat swinging her up the
steps to his house, fumbling for a key in his jacket that she
was wearing, making her giggle as he lifted a knee to
balance her while patting the jacket pocket, the pocket
which was slung low at her hip, and reaching in for the
key. I will remember being disgusted and bruised and
bitter.

My memory will be faulty. I will look back and think
generously that she was in the right place, that Sam was
looking after her, that her injuries would be healed and of
course she needed to be grateful to her rescuer. However,
at the time I thought nothing of the sort. I just seethed and
raged all night, even angrier that there was nothing in the

house to drink, banging on the door of The Naval Volunteer after closing time and walking down to the beach to sit and glower at the rusted moon.

Samuel Tempest
2nd June 1912
Sussex Coast

It has been stifling and airless for days and I want to be at sea. I've been stuck in the workshop and crew room of the lifeboat house all day thinking of her face when I pulled her out of the water. I need a callout to take my mind off her. I'm getting all moony like Wilf, it's not good for me. I keep thinking about her eyes as I carried her into the house and bathed her cuts. Her winces and the tear escaping form the corner of her eye, then the smile again.

She slept as if in a permanent dive, on her left side, with her head thrust back and her back arched. Her body lay in a soft curve, both arms above her head, the covers thrown off in the heat of the night. I lay on the floor and watched her and then when the floor rubbed my hips and shoulders I got up and sat in the wing-backed chair, feet up on the ottoman at the bottom of the bed, and watched and slept a little.

The light pushed its way through the curtains and I woke with a crick in my neck and spikes in my stomach. When I saw her on the bed, lying on her back and her arms flat out like the figure head of a ship, the spikes jabbed more furiously.

When she woke there was no start of surprise or shock. Her eyes did not flit around the room wondering where she was. She just smiled again as if she expected to wake here all the time.

'So it wasn't a dream.'

'Or a nightmare,' I said

'Nonsense.' She stretched then winced and patted her head tentatively.

I leaned towards her from the chair, conscious that my

shirt was rumpled and wishing I had washed and changed before she woke instead of sitting and gazing at her.

'Come on, it must have been terrifying. It was frightening enough for me.'

She just looked at me amused.

'I'm very grateful Sam.'

'I didn't mean that. I just meant,' but I wasn't sure exactly what I meant. 'Would you like some breakfast?' She nodded, smiling again with her eyes not her mouth.

'If you're that grateful you could come out to dinner with me tonight.' I thought I'd chance it.

'I have a diving show to do remember?'

'Not with that gash.'

'Really?'

'Really.'

She followed me downstairs and I put the kettle on the stove, lit the gas and rummaged in the bread bin. I was nervous about the state of the place, it could do with a clean. I should have got up ahead of her and at least tidied.

She sat at the table and looked up at me through her eyelashes.

'So I shouldn't do the show tonight?' There's a challenge in her voice. 'Just because you said so.'

'Because you shouldn't get that cut wet.'

'It's nothing.'

'Because I'd like to take you out to dinner.'

'There's no need.'

'Because it will be more dramatic if you cancel the show due to injury. Imagine how many people will be queuing up next time to see if you're still alive.' I turn from spooning tea into a pot to look at her over my shoulder and she is smiling broadly.

'Fine. Where are you taking me?'

Outside the seagulls are fighting over a fish, waking me from my reverie. The trawlers must be on their way in. I

33

look round the crew room. It's pretty basic really, just a place out of the weather to wait, to brief and debrief, to drink, read papers, talk about the latest rescue, while we clean the boat, while Wilf tinkers with the engine.

Wilf.

I hadn't thought about Wilf. I've been too busy thinking about Stella. He will, of course, be mad with me and accuse me, if I can get any words out of him at all, of stealing his girl. But it's only dinner, if he wants to ask her out he can.

FIVE

Stella Maris
3rd June 1912
Sussex Coast

In years to come I'm sure I'll still think of this day. I started it waking in a man's bed and then arguing with him about closing my dive show so that he could take me out to dinner. Unheard of, me closing my show for a man, but he had rescued me and when I woke this morning my head was still thumping and sore and I was secretly glad of the excuse.

Sam hasn't arranged to pick me up so perhaps that shiny motor isn't his. Instead he has asked me to be at his house at 7pm and I'm intrigued as to whether he's going to cook me a meal at home so I agreed. A man cooking, that has to be seen. So I'm wearing a dress for the occasion and I've taken a parasol like a real lady.

All the way there I keep thinking about the other man who visited my shows, the dark one who disappeared. I don't even know if he saw what happened. It wasn't him who leapt in and saved me. What did he do, just stand there and watch while I went under? He just seemed to turn up with the car afterwards as if he's some kind of chauffeur.

When I arrive at Sam's door there's no-one in but a note pinned to the red paintwork reads:

So you came then.

If you want to eat a meal with me
Walk as far as the eye can see
Where sand and shingle meet the shore
You'll never be left wanting more.

I'm stood on his front step laughing and looking

around, turning from his front door and gazing along Marine Road. He isn't much of a poet but I'm intrigued alright, well who wouldn't be. I would have preferred it to be his friend I'm meeting but still he does interest me. I set off in the early evening sunlight, parasol twirling. I like an adventure.

I pass the rope works, the fish market and boat yard and head out towards the beach. Where the shingle turns to sand there's still no sign of him and no sign of anywhere to eat. I lift my hem and walk towards the dunes, the stones squeaking under my feet. And there between the soft sand hills is Sam bent over a fire, a pan resting on the burning logs and a toasting fork in his hand. He looks up, red in the face, and waves the fork at me, his hair the colour of newly sawn wood in the evening sunlight.

He walks up to me and takes my arm without saying a word and leads me to a place a little apart from the fire where he has set a low table with a coloured cloth. There are roses in a small crystal vase and china brought from home. He seats me in a low chair, covered with cushions and rugs, its legs deep in the sand, and hands me a glass.

It's perfect. The whole evening is perfect. We eat oysters and whitebait, fried in butter, with lots of salt and pepper and thick bread and butter and we drink Guinness cooled in a metal bucket of seawater. Later, we dance to the music in our heads, a kind of waltz with Sam stumbling over his big feet, as the herringbone sky turns dark.

Stella Maris
July 12th 1912
Sussex Coast

In the mornings before I need to think about setting off for the diving show I wander down to the boatshed after I've done as many womanly, housey tasks as I can stomach. Clearing the breakfast things and a quick sweep of the floor is about all I can muster. I'm still here, the gash on my head a pale pink line.

I take a pad and pencil and sit and watch Sam at work. Sam sawing wood, shirt off, the muscles in his arms round and taut as I sketch him. I half face out of the workshop pretending I'm drawing seemly things like boats and water and gulls when I'm more interested in muscle and sinew.

Sometimes his friend Wilf comes over and leans against the doorway, smoking. I draw him as well, the way he leans his weight on one hip, the smile that gradually moves across his lips as I draw. He knows I'm drawing him. I can tell he enjoys the attention. Sam seems completely oblivious to it, absorbed in his boat, more tuned in to the lines and edges of the wood than to what we are doing. So Wilf and I communicate in a mix of smiles, half smiles and looks. Sometimes I show him what I've been drawing and he moves over to where I'm sat and stands close, too close, so close I can breathe him in and all the time he's smiling so much I can't think straight. He knows what he's doing.

Today Wilf is not with us. It is peaceful in workshop until the damn maroon goes off. Sam flies around in a flurry of sawdust, brushing wood curls from his hair. He grabs his jacket even though it is hot and the dust from his hair dances in the sunlight.

'Where the hell is Wilf?'

He looks anxiously up and down Marine Road but there is no sign of Ophelia's shining fenders.

'I'll have to go. If he doesn't get here we'll just have to go without him. Lock up for me love,' and he throws me the keys and is off at a run towards the lifeboat house.

I wait. I don't lock up straight away or run to follow him and watch them go out. It's peaceful here, no rhythmic sounds of machinery and the dust slowly settling. It must be cooler inside in the shade but I can still feel perspiration on my neck. The sun bounces off the metal.

Then there's a roaring engine and a screech of brakes. Wilf leaps from the car and is in the workshop.

'He's gone; if you hurry you might just catch them.' And I expect him to be off without a word but he just stands there, one hand on the door jam, breathing heavily.

'Wilf, they won't have gone yet', I urge. Both of us stay rooted to the spot, the band-saw between us. Sam's tools are scattered on the wooden bench. Above us hang the ribs of boats suspended in the shafts of light coming in from the roof. The room is full of light and shadow, Wilf is silhouetted, his back against the open doorway. I can feel his breathing. He pushes the door a little further to and moves closer, his footsteps softening on the ringlets of wood. He walks round the workbench and leans against it with one hip. I can see him half smile down at me and I feel my breathing quicken.

'Strawberry?'

I must be frowning, confused. He reaches into a paper bag he is carrying and pulls out a strawberry, removes the stem with his teeth, reaches forward and places the fruit into my parted lips. I bite into the flesh, the juice runs down my chin and drops fall onto my white blouse. He runs his finger over my jaw wiping away the juice and I want his finger to be his tongue.

Then there is a monstrous flapping and yaking and through the doorway a seagull swoops, huge and flailing and terrified. Its wings whirling like sails, wildly slashing at the deck. It hacks around the workshop in a frenzy, crashing its white wings against the tools, smashing into the band-saw, tearing its breast across the teeth. Wilf tries to scare it out and I'm screaming and we're caught up in a tunnel of sound and white feathers and red blood.

Stella
July 13th 1912
Sussex Coast

From the harbour arm the fishermen cast out and children

38

dangle single lines into the sea. To the west a dark space on the water is flicking, flecks of silver, tiny leaping specs, shifting like smoke clouds or like the starlings that circle the pier. The whitebait rush panicked into the shore, chased by shining black mackerel, racing unseen through the water, slipping smooth and glossy through the waves, mouths open, rounding on the whitebait, corralling them, penning them in.

I can't stop thinking about Wilf. The look in his eyes that day in the workshop, the touch of his fingers on the line of my jawbone, my throat. The seagull, the panic, the blood. My heart is beating quickly but there is no danger of it being heard. Shrieking above the mackerel there is a mob of crazed gulls, diving and harassing the fish. Dive bombing, raid after raid. Seagulls are chasing mackerel, chasing whitebait all moving towards the beach.

I find it hard to look at Sam and I wonder if it is guilt or that he is beginning to irritate me. Seeing the commotion he grabs a bucket and runs off down to the beach yelling, 'Fish for tea Stella and it's not even Friday.'

'Don't take that one; it has a hole in it.'

'There's a hole in my bucket, dear Stella, dear Stella,' and he runs to the beach anyway.

I follow more slowly. About a dozen men, women and children have gathered with buckets and nets and anything to scoop up fish. Sam smiles over his shoulder at me and digs a hole in the stones.

He jumps back as the tide rushes in bringing with it panicking, flashing fish. Everyone is rushing now in a frenzy, fish flapping, people screaming, the seagulls swoop only ten yards out. Everyone has buckets of struggling fish, too many to eat and no way of storing them and they are laughing holding bags and jackets, anything that will hold their prey. Sam holds up his bucket triumphant and the water pours from the hole in its base leaving piles of writhing, dying creatures. It is pure greed, obscene. Unless they raid the ice house there is no way of keeping the fish fresh, no way of eating enough, even the gulls are heavy and low in the sky now, skimming the waves, cumbersome with feeding. I turn and fight my way back from the people, clutching my stomach.

By the weekend the streets are filled with rotting fish in boxes, uneaten, the gulls hungry once more dive again and again pulling the flesh apart scattering the remnants across the road.

SIX

Stella Maris
18th August 1912
Sussex Coast

I watch him breathing lightly, shallowly in the early hours. Sam pulls away from the depths of his dreams, no longer battling with a rescue but calm now. His fair hair falling over his forehead just a little too long, his cheek creased from the pillow, his chest rising evenly.

Thwmp.

He is awake and my heart sinks through the bedsprings.

Crack.

His eyes flash and he has rolled over, kissed me clumsily and is out of bed, pulling on his trousers. By the Hiss, like the sound of a sash window being opened, he is at the door grinning at me, elated and apologetic at the same time. But elation wins out.

He doesn't hear the second maroon.

One
He is out of the door and down the stairs.

Two
I can see him in my mind, he'll be at the back door now.

Three
Running through the garden.

Four
Stopping at the privy to pee.

Five

Six
Across the scrubland before the river.

Seven
When I get to seven I get out of bed.

Eight
I'm at the window pulling back the curtain, wrapping the lace net around my body like a veil.

Nine
He turns from the river wall and waves.

Ten
He turns and carries on.

I see them all running, Jacky Prentice, Ted Temple, Stormy, Stan and Jerry LeBurn. I open the window and let in the morning sun, soft into the room. I breathe in the summer. I hear Wilf's car screeching to a halt and I can see him in my head leaping over the driver door and I want to cry.

Samuel Tempest
18th August 1912
The English Channel

Wilf is yelling, sitting in Ophelia, engine running, hooting the horn at me in one continuous frustrated blast.

'Why do ships have to always choose such damn inconvenient times to get into trouble?' I pretend to grumble as I run to the boat.

'I can always take your place as Coxswain if you want to go and play with your girly.' Wilf leaps from Ophelia. I ignore him. He grabs his jacket from the back seat and slams her door. His jacket catches and rips as he rushes away. He swears.

We arrive at the lifeboat house at the same time as Jacky. He grins, leaping on board first as if to make a point.

'Finished all that damn fish now?' Wilf mutters without looking at me.

'It was great thanks.'

'Did you need quite so much of it?' He leaps on board

and starts throwing kit around. He's rattled. I'm sure he would have had his fair share of fish if he'd been there.

'You could've had some; just because I got there first.' Ted and Stan are running down the quay and Stormy is already throwing on his sou'wester and strapping on his life jacket.

Wilf is at the engine, 'You don't even like mackerel. It's all just for bloody show isn't it?'

I start yelling my instructions to the crew even before I get on The *Lucy May*.

'Come on lads, I know it's early but let's focus.' We're all on board now and ready for the launch. 'What the hell's wrong with you this morning?' I snap at Wilf just as Jerry swipes out the holding pin. Wilf, moody and spiky, breathes comments under his breath as we slide backwards down the slipway.

'Sweet Jesus, why do we need to go in backwards?' Wilf moans as he tries to crank the engine. I glance at him out of the corner of my eye but he is already at the engine and doesn't notice.

'Because the skipper says so,' Ted says grinning and nodding towards me. I'm on my feet and scanning the horizon.

'Awkward bugger. Anything for a show for the on-lookers, any sane coxswain would do down forwards.' Wilf is clearly in a mood with me, but he'll have to get over it. We have a job to do.

We plunge into the waves. They surge up the deck and the shock of them in the heat makes us gasp. Exhale. Breathe, keep breathing.

Everyone seems to be listening for my instructions except Wilf who is still muttering under his breath.

'Come on Wilfred we don't want to be rowing,' I say, knowing I'll wind him up. Ted and Stormy haul up the mainsail and we flounder somewhat until the engine coughs and the familiar rub and thrum of it sings out.

Turning out of the harbour we can see the trail of smoke

from the cargo steamer, beckoning us like a beacon. As we near the ship my heart starts to race. The size of it, the looming bulk of it. A two hundred foot cargo ship listed so severely to port that the rails are deep in the waves. She sways at an angle of forty-five degrees. The crew, perching on the guard rail above the accommodation, get a foothold where they can. The lifeboat is insignificant next to the bulk of this ship, corklike and bobbing. My crew fall silent, I try to think. The engine throbs, gently motored down. The ship's chief mate is shouting but his English is poor, I've no idea what nationality they are, the lettering on the hull spells out *Koning William 111*. I look around but my crew shrug unhelpfully and the chief mate's words are torn away by the screeching gulls.

These damn gulls seem to have followed us out and they swim in the grey clouds haunting the stricken vessel. As the sun leaves the shelter of the clouds it catches the white paint on the hull of the ship and the dull steel is suddenly illuminated with a flash of silver sending out its SOS to the shore.

The lifeboat creeps closer. We have fallen silent and watchful, the deck climbs away like the face of Beachy Head itself. Wilf emerges blinking from the engine's embrace, away from the hum and vibration and scent of petrol and shakes himself into this world of swell and air and pariah gulls. I close my eyes and I'm aware of Wilf taking the helm. I let him so that I can concentrate, balancing like a dog in a cart, leaning into the turn and bracing my legs with each rise and fall.

Opening my eyes I notice the accommodation of the ship. A crew member and what looks like the Captain are struggling with a door which is closed and at a sharp angle. They are desperately pulling but cannot move it. Nestled in the crook of deck and accommodation bulkhead, balanced in the V, they pull against themselves but the weight of the door, the lean of the ship, the heave and pitch of the swell, keeps the door tight shut. Stormy passes me the telescope pointing. I focus it on who I believe to be the Captain and see the desperate look on his face. His thoughts are clearly not with the vessel or the crew but with whatever precious cargo is stowed behind the jammed door.

And then I stir from the depths of my thoughts.

'The cargo has shifted. Can we see what she's carrying?'

I pass the telescope to Ted who focuses it quickly. I'm fully awake now and steadying the tiller again, squinting at the deck. My crew watch, listening to the sounds of our own breath, the wash of the swell, the hum of the motor. Occasionally there is the wheel and cry of the gulls and the terrible creaks of the silver vessel. Then a crack as something huge shifts its weight.

Wilf has spotted that we need to move The *Lucy May* and quickly. We are too close to the shifting cargo, if it comes away, breaks its lashings and slides towards the sea we will all be crushed.

I spin the boat around; we're in the lee of the ship, the sheltered side but perilously close the shifting cargo. I ready Wilf and Stormy to go aboard.

'We have to jettison the cargo. Ted, can you see what they're carrying now?'

'It looks like planks of wood strapped to the deck and crates as well, there's no telling what's in those.'

Wilf and Stormy are on the edge of the lifeboat, I bring her as close as I dare so that they can jump aboard. I try not to think of what will happen if our small boat gets caught under the ship or if they don't make it but we've done this so often. It's just what we do.

Wilfred Kay
18th August 1912
The English Channel

Have I explained about the fear of the space between two boats? Let me just say that every sailor has a terror of the gap between hulls. I don't swim: a good swimmer is a bad sailor, but my fear of the water is nothing in comparison to my terror of that space. Some are afraid of fire at sea but fire is pretty rare, and there is always the sanctuary of the waves. Some fear the tearing wind and the damage it can bring, dragging boats off course, sending masts crashing and sails ripping, but worse than these nightmares are the yawning gaps between boats. The gaps between them when they rise and fall like horses on a carousel. One rising as the other sinks. Crossing between the two is all in the timing. You have to leap when your boat is slightly higher. Some lifeboat men make it look as simple as stepping out for a walk in the country. There must to be no hesitation, not for a moment. If you miss your chance you have to wait for the next swell and by then you may have lost your bottle. So you stand on the precipice staring at the gnawing waves, counting, timing and then leap. Of course it's fine if the boats are both small but when one is vast in comparison to the lifeboat it becomes terrifying. To be caught between two boats, the barnacled sides of two boats, the seaweed softly disguising the teeth on the boat's belly. To lose your foothold and slip down between two crushing, rubbing, grinding hulls.

I wait for The *Lucy May* to rise just above the rail of the ship and close my eyes just for a moment. I cut out Sam and my anger. I see Stella. I'm sure that this wouldn't frighten her. She would revel in the adventure and would not think of the sliding metal below. But I have to stop thinking of Stella and get on with it.

The ship looms towards me, an angle of shining, swelling, slipping wood and metal. How to get a grip on such a sliding hulk of a thing? How to land and look confident to the crew whose eyes have clouded over and whose captain is frantic at the door of the cabin?

'Now,' and Stormy and I leap and scramble over the guard rail and onto the angled deck of the ship. I look up at the crew teetering above. One of them throws a line down and the sopping coil of rope whips at my face before landing at my feet. Then another for Stormy and we use them to scramble up the incline, half hauled by the crew.

'What's your cargo?' Stormy shouts to the chief mate who looks as if this is a ridiculous question but answers, 'Teak and typewriters.'

Teak and typewriters. This cannot be real. I feel as if I am in some kind of dream. What ship carries teak and typewriters?

'We're going to have to jettison some of it to right her,' I don't wait for a response but the mate is motioning to the release hooks.

'They must be jammed.' Stormy says and I wonder why they haven't taken a sledgehammer to them already. Perhaps the Captain's fear has paralysed the crew as well. If we don't do something the ship will list so far over they will not be able to be saved and the Captain is doing nothing about it.

Stormy rigs up a system of ropes to lower me back down the incline of the deck to cut free the teak stacked there. To free the crates and send typewriters spinning into the sea, ribbons flying, keys chattering like teeth, return carriages pinging. He lowers me down. I hang onto the rope with him guiding me, hauling me up when the bottom crates are shifted. The wood snaps and scatters into the sea.

I hover with my knife poised over the lashings and I can see the Captain. A tall man, the height of the cabin door but withered somehow from the inside out, his face creasing like a paper bag, his fists curling inward as they pound. I release the teak and we surge upward, the ship jerkily righting itself with every load that slams into the waves. The Captain heaves again at the door. Then I'm aware of something behind me and Sam has given the helm to Ted. Sam stands, seemingly watching the ship rise and fall. I squint and see that his eyes are closed as if in prayer but if Sam is praying it will be Poseidon and Thor, to the ancient gods of the sea and sky. And then he

47

is awake again and waving at Stormy who has abandoned me and is busy organising the crew to throw a line down to haul Sam up the deck. What the hell is he doing? For God's sake Sam we don't need any of your heroics now. I bite my lip and let another load go just as Sam leaps so that he lands awkwardly and is flung up the deck with the lurch of the ship. He grabs the line thrown down to him, panic crosses his wide open face like a cloud but only for a moment and he is waving and shouting again.

And then I feel terrible and am muttering, 'Holy Mary Mother of God why did I do that?' but it's something to do with him leaving The *Lucy May* again, leaving his crew. Something to do with him thinking I cannot handle this, that I'm not capable of righting this ship, that I wouldn't get onto the problem with the Captain as soon as the ship was more stable. It's obvious to me that the door he is hammering on won't open until the ship is more level. Why can't he wait and let me do it for once? Is the damned glory all he wants? I'm frustrated because for once I can't be there to back him up and bail him out, because I'm dangling on a damned rope off the side of this lurching ship. And it's something to do with him rescuing my girl on the night when I was going to make a move, something to do with the look in her eyes as she gazed up at him from the sopping wet pier.

He's on board now and it's easier than when we leapt across. The ravine between the boats is not so pronounced, the ship is more level thanks to our efforts. Stormy is back with me, guiding me to the next crate. We must've shifted tonnes of cargo, just a few more crates in the sea and we might be able to open the cabin door.

I'm not sure if I have closed my eyes and pictured it all or whether I am watching it happen but the next thing is that my crate crashes down the incline, spilling its load and smashing into the water. Sam climbs towards the cabin, catapulted upward as the crate leaves the deck. He reaches the distraught captain, hauls open the door, with the help of the next jolt, and emerges carrying a wailing baby with its mother hanging onto his arm. It's like a scene from a film, or the end of a novel. The Captain falls on his wife and child and the crew surround Sam and I want to retch.

After that I don't want to remember much, Stormy has lost his concentration, caught up with the jubilation on deck. I look down and see The *Lucy May* bobbing nearby, just standing by, waiting. I have the old fear of the gap between boats. It swells up in me again.

Sam is shouting needless instructions to Ted at the helm of The *Lucy May*. No-one seems to be watching how dangerously close the ship is to the lifeboat. And with neither the coxswain nor second coxswain aboard she is short of a leader. There's a horrible scraping, Ted's face seems to white out in panic. He wrestles with the helm but The *Lucy May* is ripped by the *Koning William III*, sheared into. Our crew are knocked flat with the impact. Then the line I'm attached to catches on some cargo and, without Stormy watching, shears off. I slam into the water. It's freezing. I don't swim and I want to drown quickly before one of the vessels bears down and traps me but I don't drown and the crush, when it comes, is too much to bear.

SEVEN

Stella Maris
18th August 1912
Sussex Coast

When they're on a callout I go into an automatic routine. I cannot think of Wilf and Sam, Sam and Wilf both on The *Lucy May*. But she will look after them. I am sure of it.

I wash, tipping water from the jug into the basin, lathering soap in a rhythmic motion, refusing to think. I can see them leaping onto the boat.

How can I say what it is like to be left behind, to wait while they are the ones at the action? Time flies for them. Keyed up, they often return high and happy and full of stories. They've no idea what it's like to be the one left behind, the one who has to watch and to wait. So I think about their elation, about Sam's excited chatter, about Wilf's silent smile. I do not think of what happens if something goes wrong. They are fine boat men. Sam is a good skipper; he has Wilf to back him up.

It seems that I think about both of them, worry about both of them, both in the same thought, the same breath. Sam's been getting on my nerves lately. He's so gung ho about things. More and more my thoughts turn to Wilf but I feel a loyalty to Sam. He did rescue me after all which is more than I can say for Wilf.

I dress. Pulling on a skirt or trousers, Sam likes me to wear a skirt so I usually wear trousers out of devilment but they are feeling tight so today I reach for a skirt. Then a blouse, whatever is to hand. The clothing is tight around my belly and the buttons on the blouse strain a little across my breasts. My nipples are so firm at the moment that if I brush through doorways I think I'm going to chip the paintwork. Sam jokes that they are like Ophelia's

50

wheel nuts but he's not complaining, he seems to like them well enough.

I throw open the windows and gulp in the air.

Pour water into a bucket.

Wash the floor.

Wash the windows.

Wash the walls.

Biting back my fear, drowning it in water, cleansing it. I wash and change water and rinse until my knuckles are sore and my skin wrinkled and red.

The sky is muddied and the air heavy. Lazy bees bump the glass as I pour vinegar onto newspaper and rub and shine, rub and shine the windows. I can feel them coming home, Sam joking about it being a good job there's a call-out otherwise the house would never get cleaned. I'm never sure whether to enjoy the joke or not.

They are still not back and the air is so heavy there is no relief. There's a dull pain in the bottom of my stomach like the damned curse. In the garden I pick the thorns methodically off the roses. I start at the top of the stem where the thorns are new and harmless, running them over the pad of my thumb before flicking them off. Down the stem to the tougher ones beneath, picking them off and sending them spinning like tiny sharks teeth into the earth below. Digging them under my nail, seeing how far I can push it, the delicious pain of the skin under the nail being pushed, spiked down until the pain is no longer pleasurable. It's like wiggling a loose tooth or pressing a nail into candle wax, exhilarating and sore at the same time.

I think of them at sea. I go through the motions in my head, feeling every wave break over the bow of The *Lucy May*. Sam at the helm, Wilf at his side coaxing the engine. I push the thorn in until it draws blood and with an irritated jerk I withdraw my finger and flick away the thorn, put my finger to my mouth and suck out the blood from under the nail.

I walk out of the house, with its shining sashes and scrubbed stone flags, past the pots with tumbling geraniums, still sucking my finger. By now I should be getting ready for my first show of the day. All I can think of is the water. Over the river a turn flicks and skims across the river, black head flashing, whiter and cleaner than any washing soap ever gets clothes. It jerks back and enters the water with an untidy plash, up again, something shiny and wriggling in its beak.

The barnacled struts of landing stages reach out across the river. I kick off my shoes and walk out on one of the wooden bars. It is covered in a fine and smooth seaweed like baby's hair, slippery, glossy between my toes. The wood is like a diving platform and I jump in a clean arch, my skirt swinging around my legs. I cleave through the water clean and sweet.

Opening my eyes I see bubbles and the light kalidescoping the rocks and reed. Shoals of tiny fish flash silver through the weed and I swirl around the limbs of the fishing pontoon, dancing with it in a slow tango before bursting to the surface. A gulp of air and under again swimming down, floating in circles, somersaulting in amniotic fluid, kicking and gurgling. Holding my belly in glee.

'Stella.'

Running out of air.

'Stella.'

Heading for the surface.

'Ste-lllaaa.'

The gorgeous feeling of not having enough air, lungs squeezed out, all the dead stale air pressed out of the body, the brain screaming for oxygen, the risk of it, the wonderful crush and rush of it.

Into the air, head flung back.

'Stella, they're back.' And young Alfie LeBurn, Jerry's boy, is hopping about on the jetty calling my name and pointing at the lifeboat.

The *Lucy May* is reeling through the water, heeling over

with a heart stopping gash in her hull. A bite out of the wood as if a huge sea creature has gorged itself on her. And they are rowing.

Exhausted.

I am pulling myself out of the water, wading to the rocks and scrambling over them, running, skirt sticking to my legs, water streaming down my thighs, my neck, my arms, and I'm crying already. Great silent sobs. I try to count them as I run, Jacky, Ted, Stan but I keep missing them as they rise and fall.

'Alfie, can you count them?'

'I have five.'

'Oh God, where is he?'

'It's all right Stella, I can see him.' Alfie is pointing to a figure in the bottom of the boat. Sam kneeling. My heart jolts. Thank God. But where is he?

Silently under my breath 'Please God where is he?'

The *Lucy May* is coming alongside and there is shouting and confusion, old Jerry catching the line as Ted throws it and the boat comes flat in the water. As soon as it does water starts pouring in through the gash.

I'm kneeling on the jetty, sobbing. My stomach lurching. Sam is out of the boat and at me, gathering me up, but he doesn't say it's alright, everything is fine. I know something has happened to Wilf and I want to hit Sam, to hurt him, to bite and draw blood for hurting me, for leaving me, for letting harm come to Wilf and I sink in his arms, battering his shoulders with the palms of my hands.

EIGHT

Stella Maris
19th August 1912
Sussex Coast

He gave me brandy, supposedly to help me sleep, but it just made me more manic. I cried myself into a sick mess with eyes so puffed I could have done a few rounds with a prize fighter. My breathing became so laboured I was having convulsions which turned into hiccoughs which at any other time would have made me laugh and which would have unlocked the barrier which had slammed between us.

I lay on the bed and let Sam fuss around fanning me and bringing me more brandy which I drank quickly, enjoying the stinging glow as it slid down but it was gone too soon and left no lasting pleasure. Since it was supposed to help me sleep and as I could not face him I closed my eyes and pretended to drift off, my still burning cheek against cool cotton.

I keep thinking about the wonderful things that Sam has, his own house with lincrusta lining the walls in patterns of Greek looking urns. There are fireplaces in every room, a beautiful range which shines darkly. And then I wonder what Wilf has. He has a car. A beautiful car I admit and he works on the railway, respectable enough but not exactly his own business like Sam. Wilf is always at someone else's beck and call and isn't independence everything? Sam is independent after all and doesn't need to rely on anyone else. I turn over to find a cool piece of bed linen. These things are important to me, self reliance, independence, but all the time I cannot stop thinking about Wilf's eyes.

I pretend to sleep too long even though I don't feel as if

I have slept at all. My eyes sting and my skin feels greasy. My hip bones ache where they have dug in to the mattress and the counterpane is rough against my cheek. There's a dull pain in my belly low down near my thighs and my breasts feel bursting, my nipples hard. And now I know that I am stuck and this is where I stay no matter what I think about Wilf and his eyes.

When I do get out of bed I press a muslin dipped in water to my eyes. Breakfast is difficult. Sam acts as if nothing has happened. He prattles on about the business, about the rescue, some of the rescue. Wilf will be fine he says, just one of those things, every lifeboat man has accidents, he should learn to swim.

I let him talk, he fills my silences with words. He wants to talk about it to purge it from his mind, to cleanse himself. I think that if he is so desperate for absolution he should get a priest but of course the suggestion would send him reeling. I think about commenting but before I can he's off again: if Wilf had solved the problem faster he wouldn't have had to get involved, if Wilf had got back up the boat and out of the way, on and on and on.

But the way I see it, it's the things we cannot control and cannot see that exert their power over us, the wind, the turbulence that whips up the sea, the feelings you cannot alter, the pull of the moon. The baby rolling in my stomach.

Wilfred Kay
1st October 1912
Sussex Coast

The pain isn't so bad now. My leg is mashed up a bit but I'll be walking again before long. A few prayers to St. Joseph will put me right, he hasn't failed me yet. There's some good news though, I might have a smashed up leg but there's a rumour we're getting awards for bravery for saving the *Koning William III*.

The thing that's killing me at the moment is Stella's

news. It's not that I don't want her to be a mother but I thought all the time they weren't married there might be some chance and now I see that chance has disappeared. But I try to stay chipper. She visits as often as she can with her glowing cheeks and blooming belly and breasts.

Stella Maris
5th August 1914
Sussex Coast

> One Two, Buckle my Shoe,
> Patter cake, patter cake,
> Lavender's blue.

The words mix and muddle. I don't remember the rhymes, just snatches and phrases. My baby, our baby is a marvel. I have a baby, almost a little girl now. I can hardly believe it. She sits in front of the fireplace on a rug playing with the pegs, banging them, patting them and hugging them. Her tiny brilliant white teeth gnawing ineffectually at them. I don't know the rhymes but she doesn't care, she just smiles and smiles. Her cheeks dimpling, her hair raised up in a question mark on top of her head. I've had to stop feeding her now, those teeth diamond sharp were drawing blood and even I thought that enough was enough. When she sucked from my nipple her hands squeezed my breast, she reached up to my face as I gently rubbed my cheek over her fingers. She cupped my chin with her tiny hand and put her fingers in my mouth. I sucked them as she suckled me until her eyes folded shut.

Sam is a good father, of course he is. I mean he doesn't know anything about babies but then nor do I. He is more used to wrestling with wood and water than this pliable, soft wriggling thing that slips through his fingers. Like paying out rope she slides to the floor and kicks joyfully like summer waves rolling onto the beach. Then she's dragging herself up on to her hands and knees trying to stand.

We've been talking about her christening. Sam isn't keen because he doesn't believe in all that mumbo jumbo but he thinks it's the right thing to do and he's keen on the party and the fuss. But I doubt any priest will christen Lily with her parents unmarried. We both wear wedding rings to stop people gossiping, I don't care if they talk about me but Sam hates it, but the ring doesn't mean anything to me.

There's a wail and I rush to her. She is lying flat on her tummy with the up-turned peg basket, pegs everywhere, legs flailing and fists hovering over the rug. Her face is red and creased and cross. I swing her high into the air almost up to the ceiling rose and she cackles. I am about to lift her again when I see him outside the window finishing a cigarette, walking up and down on the path. He has something of a limp now after his accident but he's turned it in to a kind of swagger and I like it. He looks up and smiles quietly through the window, waggles his fingers at Lily.

My stomach fizzes and I go to the door, pulling my hair out of Lily's fists and wishing I had put it up. He's leaning against the wall at the top of the steps.

'Come out with me.' It's more a soft command than a question.

'Wilf, I can't. I have Lily.'

'Well bring Lily,' and he lifts out his hands to take her. She is all kicking legs and he snuggles her to him, pushes his face into her hair and breathes her in.

'And Sam?'

'Sod Sam, come on.'

Ophelia waits panting, on the road anxious to be off and I hold Lily tightly on my knee as the car springs forward with a roar. Lily's eyes blink in the cool rushing air.

'Do you want a go?' Wilf looks at me sideways smiling. He knows I can't wait to try. He places my hand on the gear lever and puts his hand, warm over mine. His fingers run over my knuckle, I turn my hand over and he caresses my palm, my wrist. We climb out of the town and up to the downs above where he brings Ophelia to a halt, jumps out and reaches for Lily.

'Your turn,' he says and I scramble across into the driving seat before he has chance to change his mind. He reaches across me to show me how to hold the steering wheel, completely needlessly, and I feel his warmth falling across my body.

'You know we may have to go Stella.' I ignore him because I don't want to think about it. Why does he have to spoil this moment?

'I'm going to try and stay here but you know Sam, he'll be off.'

'I know, he thinks it will all be over by Christmas. Idiot,' I spit out the words. Lily wriggles and babbles in Wilf's arms.

'But everyone thinks it Stell, maybe we will be home for roast turkey, perhaps they are right.'

'Don't be ridiculous Wilf, this has been brewing for months and you'll all go and you won't come back and Sam just thinks he can race around letting off a few bombs as if they are maroons and it will all be heroic and wonderful.'

'I'll do my best to look after him.'

'You always bloody well look after him. Who the hell is going to look out for you?' I'm shaking now and crying, 'how am I going to get you back?'

Lily stretches and yawns. Wilf buries his face in her warm neck, he holds my hand very tight and kisses Lily's head. Later when he passes her back to me the scent of him still lingers in her hair.

NINE

Wilfred Kay
November 1914
Northern France

'Come on lads, keep the home fires burning and all that piffle.' He doesn't notice but a couple of the lads snigger behind his back and I want to lay them out but then sometimes he deserves it. What they don't realise is that he'd lay his life on the line for them and he barely knows them. He'd probably lay half the platoon's lives on the line for them come to think of it and somehow we'd get through. In the real world we would anyway. It's just that here things are so much more unpredictable even than the English Channel and I don't think he's quite realised it yet.

We're digging ourselves in. I thought these damn trenches were already dug but apparently not so. I pull some energy from somewhere and get my back stuck into it. Sam remains cheerful as ever but I've noticed a change in him. He keeps trying to hold us together but Ted and Stormy are already off on another mission. Makes it sound exciting doesn't it? It'll be about as riveting as this one. Sam finds it hard to handle, that they are not here on his ship. They should be in this ditch with us as far as he's concerned, rocking around the French countryside being buffeted by the elements but they have already gone overboard and no amount of heroics will keep them within sight. And Jacky, so clumsy that Sam feels he needs to keep him on a leash. Then there are all of the other crew members who have joined us on this journey. The rest of the lads that Sam is attempting to keep aboard, most of them couldn't give a toss and are already floundering and drowning. That's the difference between us. He can enjoy life but as soon as there's a callout, or a mission of some sort, he forgets everything else. He has focus. My mind is everywhere, with Stella mainly. I can get lost in my thoughts and forget what I'm doing. Sam never does. But there's already a change in him, he has no control over the situation we're in and I can see him getting less buoyant and more miserable by the day.

And of course he's out of his depth. We all are. If he'd had the patience to wait we might have joined the navy and be doing something useful, something we understand. But no, Sam was joined up to the first regiment that would have him and without a coxswain we all sort of followed or were cajoled into it. That's no excuse, we made our own decisions and I promised Stella I'd watch over him so here I am watching him make a damn fool of himself and miles away from any sea.

A couple of the lads stop digging and light up cigarettes while the corporal isn't looking and I can see Sam reddening in fury. At the beginning I would have put a hand on his shoulder to calm him but now I don't care. He winds me up. I wouldn't mind so much if he were doing it all for Stella but of course he isn't. I wonder if he even remembers who Stella and Lily are. So I let him get on with it, making an idiot of himself. It might give me some satisfaction. So we dig on, Sam's eyes flash around the rest of us, checking and watching for any mishap, waiting for his moment.

Samuel Tempest
14th May 1918
Northern France

We march for what feels like forever but by the height of the sun it's probably only about three hours. My coat lies heavy on my back and the straps of the pack dig into my shoulders like a curse. We pass through scrappy farms and villages. A man cleaning the display window of a bread shop eyes us from his ladder. I didn't do much

French at school so I nod but he just keeps looking, his eyes following our line as we march past.

Heavy uddered cows graze under stubby cider trees. A big house, a chateau I suppose you would call it, overrun by the army, appears across fields. Squinting I can squeeze out the dull green trucks skewed to a halt in the drive.

There's a stop for Woodbines and water. There's a river and the men are trundling down to it, pulling off boots that are glued to their feet. Draping their legs in the water, plunging them in quick hoping that the blister pus will be washed away in the eddies. I keep my boots on. If I take them off they'll need to leave me here. My feet will balloon to twice their size and explode; it's only leather and sweat that is controlling them, keeping them from combusting.

We're off again. Grumbling, swearing, the usual round. It looks as if we're heading up there to the chateau. Straight up the drive, no sneaking round to the trades-men's entrance. There are balconies and terraces with iron tables and chairs. All we need are a few parasols.

The place is buzzing with khaki. We're sent round the back. Only officers allowed inside. A paddock, next to a tangle of raspberry and blackberry canes, holds tents in peaked rows. We are set to putting up ours. Pulling the guy ropes taught we could be on a camping holiday. We should sit round a campfire and sing.

No campfire. But we lie with our kit bags under our heads, smoking. Cigarette embers, pointing towards the stars, burn into the night. If Wilf sees me smoking I'll never live it down after all the times I've moaned at him about it. Cigarettes don't go with wood and boats but out here its different, everything is different. I'm turning into Wilf, I can feel it. I find it hard to focus and I feel as bloody morose. I haven't seen him in days now. I was concerned at first but he's been so damn sullen with me that it's been a pleasure to get away from him for a bit. I suppose all that stuff with Stella doesn't help but she could've been his girl and she chose me. But I daren't think about it too much because somewhere inside I wonder if she isn't already his girl.

There's talk of a push but there's always talk of a push. There's a buzz among the ranks. I look back at the stars. Tomorrow we are back at the front again.

The light shoves its fingers into the holes in the tent. I usually sleep poorly but last night I slept as if a drug was put in my water bottle. It's a good job because I don't sleep properly again.

I can hear the others being woken. They are almost at me with their, 'rise and shine' and worse. I see the camouflage smears staining the tent. I squint; the shapes could be figures from King Tut's tomb. A pyramid and a bird headed man almost come into focus and then the tent is rippled by a gunstock and the patterns dissolve. And we are out and packing and moving again.

The mist is dissolving between the trees, low and heavy with apples, some fallen. We step out of line to grab them, pushing the treasure into our pockets. For now the officer pretends not to see. Harry tries once too often, his apple disguising the future sting of a wasp. It angrily buzzes away. He yelps and curses and drops the apple. Someone steps on it, the wasp returns, dodging black booted feet. We tread the rotten fruit, crushing the juice; pungent it scents the air.

Within a few hours the sun is splitting the sky and greatcoats are coming off. The mist is sucked away and the stony ground pierces our feet with every footfall. And now we can hear it, the old thud and shudder of shells up at the front, comforting as a train rumbling over tracks in the night. We seem to be aiming for a building on the ridge, which looks inviting, smoke seeping from the roof. I imagine a fire for hot water and mugs of tea. As we get closer the perspective shifts and the smoke is coming from smouldering shells far behind what is obviously no more than a large barn. Now we can see the front as well as hear it.

A battalion returning from the trenches passes us. We greet them with banter at first but as the grim line snakes past we fall into silent nodding, trying not to catch their eyes. The front of the group is dishevelled, a few limping, arms in makeshift slings. As the trail moves on there is a sting in its tail. Gashed men leaning on each other, tattered, caked in mud. Eyes staring at the earth or sky. I wonder not at the wounds but at the mud. Here it's so dry, the earth baked.

At a fall back trench we stand numb from walking, the rhythm still pulsating in our heads. I see a man sway with it even though he is standing still. Like coming in from a long stint at sea, the wash still rocks you. We drop our packs, they fall like bodies onto the wooden planks of the trench.

'Now listen. Our mission is simple. It is to connect communication lines to a part of the front line trench cut off by Germans. We occupy the trench but they have taken a section of it in the middle. Our men in the east of the trench can't communicate with the ones in the west.'

The briefing is punctuated with the now familiar boom of fire. We are to tool up from the friendly sounding Crab Apple Trench, make our way along the connecting trench until we get to Gillyflower Trench on the front line. I note the smirks at the name. All we have to do is nip out of the back of the trench, run our cables along until we hit the wire line between Crab Apple and Gillyflower. We follow this until we see the Tommies and then make a dash across and in. We are to go before day break, while the Hun are still snoring. Not get involved in any real fighting. We'll be covered by riflemen in Crab Apple the whole time. It will be fine. Sharp in and out. That's the plan.

It's a good job they don't give us much time to think about it. They make it sound so easy. It's only mugs like us who have to trail wire within a few feet of the bastard enemy. If we were at sea I wouldn't think twice about any of it but here it gives me the shivers.

Then we are off to our dugouts to bed down before the pre-dawn foray.

'None of your bloody snorin' tonight, Taffy.'

'Go to hell you English bastard.'

'Tommy, would you be kind enough to have the butler give us a 5am alarm call? And kippers and kedgeree will be fine for breakfast.'

'You'll be lucky to get any kip never mind bloody kippers.'

The beds are hollowed into the walls of the dug-out, some in spaces off corridors of mud, some in small anti chambers – almost rooms.

'I'd like to introduce you to the brown room, it has a fine view of . . .'

'My backside.'

The air is greasy with the reek of feet and farts.

'Oi Boots, can we persuade you to take those clod-hoppers off?'

'It'll cost you.' There are jeers and catcalls.

I'm glad they don't use my name, my real name; I don't much feel like Samuel Tempest, boat builder, craftsman and lifeboat hero. That's another life and another me, one I hope to find again. For now I'm plain old Boots, keeping my head down, trying not to think.

We lie fully clothed and smoke, our coats thrown over us, jabbering with false bravado into the night. I close my eyes and can see stars scudding across my eyelids. Closing my eyes doesn't stop me seeing. Even in the mud I'm thinking of stars, Stella. I'm so glad you can't see me out here or hear my thoughts. I'm so damn morose most of the time you wouldn't recognise me. Maybe I'm more like Wilf than I thought.

There's hushed talking from the trench corridor. And then I'm awake and staring.

It's black in the dugout. I can't make out anything.

There are grunts above me and trumpeting snores. I sit up.

'. . . you'll be joining this party. They're resting.' There is some murmuring.

'There're a couple of spare bunks in here. We're up at 5am.'

A flashlight with a cupped hand over it, to dim the searing brightness, points the way. Two men shuffle inside, past me. They find their bunks. My heart thumps. There is some stumbling as the flashlight goes off too soon and cursing and then after more shuffling a match is struck. I turn onto my side and look through my half closed lids. Black hair, hollow cheeks flare in the light of the match and are gone. It could be anyone. I turn away from the red glow of a burning cigarette. I should feel comforted but as I turn away I can feel him boring his bayonet into my back.

5am. It's still almost black in the trench. Shouts from the officer. I'm out of the dugout quickly.

'Hey, Boots is keen.'

No sign of the two new arrivals, they must be out already. I follow the corridor squeezing past dazed men. It's like some cheap hotel where you can arrive at any time of day or night. Some who had arrived late in the dugout had crammed themselves against its wall. They were out cold. Stepping over them I head outside. Nearing the light the ground becomes sloppy. A couple of men pass me dripping. The sky is leaden and the rain is coming down in stair-rods.

We gather at the mouth of the dugout, shivering with the shock of being awake. And he is there, leaning against the sandbagged wall smoking as always. He raises an eyebrow at me. Nothing more to show he knows me and with him is Jacky Prentice, who greets me like I'm his father, beaming.

'I got separated,' he said breathlessly.

'So what's new?' I smile at Wilf but he doesn't smile back.

'But Wilf found me.'

We pass round the water bottle and eat a few dry biscuits as we receive our instructions. We gather the wire, cutters and pegs and silently head through the connection trench to Gillyflower. We step over sleeping soldiers. A few vacant-eyed sentries nod as we pass.

Corporal Hurst is assigned to us like a buddy escorting new boys at school.

'How far away are the Hun from here?' I ask.

'Not far, on a quiet night you can hear them breathing.'

I wasn't sure whether to believe him. I'm paired up with Jacky which is good, it means I can keep an eye on him and he's a butcher's son so he should be alright here.

Corporal Hurst winks, 'It's lovely sharing a trench with the Hun. They occupy the middle. It's about as near as you can get. Sort of, in front of the front line.' I look at Jacky. The rest our party shuffle along behind us.

The corporal starts walking. 'A bit tricky for our chaps at the other end though, can't communicate with them at all. That's where you lot come in.' He marches ahead perkily as if he were showing us around a stately home. Did you know that the Fortesque-Masons occupy the east wing, oh yes and some undesirable Schmits have just taken up residence in the central part. We like to keep our distance you know, try not to see too much of them, they're not our sort at all.

'We've built up an earth and sandbag wall between us and I should think they've done the same. I'll take you to the farthest extent of our trench. Then, all you need to do is hop over, round the Hun and down to our chaps at the other side, shouldn't take more than a few minutes. Just in time for breakfast.' I want to spit at him.

'It's almost dawn, won't there be a raid soon?'

'Probably, but you're here now, might as well get it over with.'

He could've been talking about a trip to the nit nurse.

Jacky raises his eyes to the heavens and they are immediately filled with rain.

There isn't too much activity at this end of the trench. We pass a sentry; he can't have been more than eighteen, leaning on the middle rungs of a ladder. His body flat to it. His eyes glued to a periscope. We squeeze past a group of earnest soldiers, muttering, gathering themselves into some ramshackle order. The corporal pushes us on with the certainty and self-importance of someone who has walked this furrow often. There is no wind, thank God, but the rain is heavier than ever. Even the corporal is slipping now and I hear Jacky cursing low under his breath behind me. Round a sharp bend a shot-away sign says: 'Do not stand about here. If you're not shot someone else will be.' I bow my head lower and hurry on. The corporal stops suddenly and we bump into each other which would be comic on a stage. No one laughs. A couple of men are desperately trying to shore up a split in the enemy side of the mud walled trench.

The water is cascading through from an old shell crater above. Automatically we start fetching and carrying sand bags. I feel like the Dutch boy. If I just fit my whole body in the wall perhaps I can stop the rush of water and they can leave me here and go and fight their war. At last we seem to have the crack plugged and we stumble on, covered in slimy mud. I wonder if we'll ever make it to the German end of the trench or whether our war will consist of wandering up and down this corridor helping a little here and there, tinkering ineffectually with whatever calamity we may come across. The corporal stops. Puts his finger to his mouth as if shushing a child.

'We need to be quiet from here,' he says but as we haven't been talking at all I can't think how to be quieter. I raise my eyes to Jacky who mouths 'wanker' at the corporal's back.

We continue. I can see what I suppose is a command post. Little more than three men, a makeshift table and a few bits of equipment. One man has ear defenders. We are introduced with waves and gestures and are ushered towards the officer.

The water, thank God, has stayed out of my boots, the thought of having to take them off to dry them out fills me with horror. It's all I can think about. Here I am a few feet from the Germans and all I can think about are my feet.

It's quiet, no firing. We line up. We'll be covered. Just a dash out of the back of the trench on the allied side towards Crab Apple. Run out the wire as we go. It'll be simple. Thread the cable along the barbed wire and head back to the Tommies sharpish. Nothing to worry about, completely routine. I'm still with Jacky. The riflemen covering us train their guns out over the top of the sandbag barrier towards the enemy. I take a ladder from the front of the trench and press it to the back wall ready. It slides around in the mud.

One of the riflemen whispers, 'We get shot for desertion if we go out that way.' But he does not turn his head and I'm not sure if he's joking. The officer peers into a cloth covered periscope and surveys the land above.

'Remember, be quick, be silent and if you get hit, roll into a shell crater and wait for the stretcher bearers.'

I feel a heat at the back of my head. No-one mentioned getting hit earlier. A voice to my left whispers, 'All clear. Go.'

We're off first with our coils of cable, up the ladder at the side of the trench. Peering over the top through the rain. The wire has been cut at the head of the ladder, a big enough gap to shove through.

Jacky is pushing behind me. I snag my face on barbs as I shove through, then I'm up and over and running out my wire. The ground is shiny from the rain sitting on the surface filling every hollow, taking too long to seep into the parched earth. I'm slipping; Jacky is behind me. I hear him sliding. We stop to push in a few pegs to secure the wire, their curling metal struts piercing the wet earth.

'Just like camping. Bash in a couple of tent pegs Jack.'

As the sky lightens I can see shadows behind us loping

through the rain. As Jacky finishes I lift my bent head and the water, caught on the rim of my helmet, gushes down my neck.

We reach the barbed wire and stop to loop the cable around it.

'Just like Christmas decorations.'

'Deck the fucking halls,' says Jacky.

We run parallel with the earth works and wire of Gillyflower. Praying the Germans are sound asleep. We tread on stuff. Bits of metal. Not long ago this was the front line. Helmets lie filling with water. Bird baths for the skylarks. Fragments of material are disappearing into the mud and for a moment I wonder what they are attached to, but only for a moment.

A whistle sizzles over my head and suddenly it's Guy Fawkes night. The Tommies' flag waves and I aim for it, Jacky on my tail. I make a dive and we are being pulled down into the trench. I stumble out of the way as Jacky slides down next to me cracking the butt of his rifle into my shoulder as he falls. The pain shoots down my arm and my fingers go numb.

'Sorry mate, did I catch you?'

I don't even get a chance to lie that it is nothing. My head is full of the crap we just missed and how the hell we're going to get back.

Time for a Woodbine and a brief shelter from the rain.

TEN

Stella Maris
May 1918
Sussex Coast

When I tell her my stories she quivers and her eyes glitter.
Lily runs and hides squealing, creeps back enchanted,
begging for more.

I tell her about the famous scientists who float in the
airships above the harbour surveying the land and sea
below. How they are searching for ancient fortresses and
underwater castles. The flares and explosions that flower
into the sky, blooming and glowing, are the firecrackers
from a lost tribe who live on an island not far from the
land. They dance their ritual dances round huge camp
fires on the beach, swishing their skirts of grasses and
breathing fire into the night. She watches the bombs with
wonder; she deliciously eats up the stories and floats
through the war wide-eyed at its delights. So convinced is
she by the tales that I am almost seduced myself and I
walk with a lighter step through the fear.

She never asks about her Daddy but I do my best to
remind her of him. Sometimes though, we are so much
together and so much alone that it is hard to remember
that there were ever three of us. Sometimes down at the
beach she waves across to France and she swears she can
see him so we wave and wave and I wave two hands, one
for Sam and one for Wilf.

So now I'm driving an ambulance. I never thought that
those moments caught with Wilf in Ophelia would
actually be useful. When he taught me the feel of the
throttle, how to control her, how to make her do what you
want. His hand covering mine over the gear lever, his
breath warm on my neck.

Lily comes out with me in the ambulance sitting up in the front seat. I've made her some little trousers to wear as well. Clambering around in a dress in an ambulance wouldn't be dignified would it? And we're not the only ones now. Mind you, it doesn't stop people staring but they can stare.

I've been writing to them both but after I've told Sam how Lily is I don't know what else to say, so my letters are short. I think, write a few lines but write often. It must be better for him if the letters keep coming, even if they are short. Better than writing lots of pointless nonsense. But when I write to Wilf I take my time. I do it late at night when Lily is asleep, I lie on the bed, stretched out, savouring every word as if he is with me and there always seems to be so much to say. I haven't mentioned the driving to Sam, I know he won't approve of a woman doing a man's work but with Wilf I can really let him know everything and pour out all the adventures Lily and I have.

Samuel Tempest
15th May 1918
Northern France

When I catch my breath the pain in my arm screams at me to give it some attention. Jacky is fumbling for a Woodbine and shielding it from the rain. His hand shakes but he turns the shake into a flick to put out the match. The cigarette goes out straight away and he has to try again. Our cables have been taken from us by a beaming corporal who seems to be gabbling but all I can hear is the rain drumming in my ears and the whiz-bangs soaring overhead. Jacky is crouching now, his hand cupped over the cigarette. Then I remember myself and haul him upright and follow the soldier with the cables along the trench. There's something about these corporals, they're all so damn cheerful. Is this what operating so near to the enemy does to you, crease a chirpy smile onto your face? The firing stops but it's still the rain that I can hear.

Everyone is up now and moving about, smoking and stamping in the puddles gathering on the duck boards. There is some frantic sandbagging to build up the lips of the dugouts.

6am or thereabouts. It should be dawn but it's so dark from the black rain clouds that it's hard to tell. It starts. I can usually focus but the noise sounds like maroons going off and it's as much as I can do not to start running for The *Lucy May*. I'm back there in a howling force eight, chopping through the channel, the rain stinging my skin, scanning the horizon for the lost ship. But it is only for a moment. The infernal battering of gunfire keeps me well and truly focused in the present. Great thuds catch me at the back of the lungs. Plumes of smoke sting my eyes.

We are connecting the wire to the field telephone and I'm trying to work with Jacky holding his helmet over me to stop the water getting in. Then there's a blast that knocks us against the wood slats. Everyone is scurrying around picking up the mud-soaked equipment, backing off down the trench away from the bit that the Hun have taken residence in. My ears are numb and the sounds are dulled so it seems as if I'm watching one of those moving pictures. No sound just mouthed words. I want to laugh but something inside won't let the laughter out.

Jacky and I gather the cables and retreat. How the hell are we going to get back to our battalion now? We don't want to be stuck in the wrong end of this trench.

Then it happens. An explosion, everyone is running. An officer organises his troops at the bottom of the ladders. Bayonets are fastened to the barrels of guns and I nod at Jacky to get out, to get back to our own battalion but we are being pushed into line. I open my mouth to protest, to say that we are bloody signallers and not part of this infantry but nothing comes out except, 'bloody signallers.'

'I agree mate, bloody signallers never do any real combat.'

I'm pushed along. I want to make a break for it, shaking with rage and indignation at the injustice of it. We're not trained to go over the top, we're signallers. I'm about to protest again but the men are on the ladder. The soldier next to me focuses his eyes on my forehead and bores them into me. I face the wall of mud and my turn.

It's a mess up here. It had been relatively quiet in the trench. Apart somehow, especially with my ears being deadened, but up here . . . There's an almighty crack, my ears are back and the sound is deafening. And I'm running forward through smoke trying to remember my basic training. I'm following Jacky. An explosion and Jacky's feet jerk up and away. I don't feel anything, just a lightness in my feet as I'm hurled in the air. Then I'm flat on my face in the mud. There's mud in my ears so the sounds are completely blocked out and I'd like to keep it that way. Mud in my eyes and caked around my teeth. I come up spluttering and spitting, blow snot and mud from my nose. I'm drowning, dirt filling up my mouth and I'm fighting to get to the surface, scrabbling for my rifle.

Silence for a few moments, then the screaming. There's too much smoke stinging my eyes. My ribs feel as if they've been sawn into with razor blades. The smoke clears a little. On my knees I head for the screaming. Crawling. My hand touches something warm. Soft. An ear. Perfectly formed and ludicrous lying in the mud. No sign of blood. Its swirls of pink skin curve out like water curling down a plughole. Then I'm at him and pulling him up. There's a bloody mess where his ear should be. He's looking at me, he doesn't take his eyes off me, and his eyes follow my every movement. The noise from the firing overpowers his screaming and his mouth is open but no sound comes out just like in the movies. Choking with shock, I drag and pull him away. For an instant I wonder about the ear. I'm in the middle of a battlefield and I'm wondering whether to pick up his damn ear from the dirt.

I stumble into more bodies but I can barely cope with Jacky. We're probably somewhere in front of the German section of the trench and I lurch blindly on not knowing where it will be safe to dive though the wire.

An enormous water-filled crater left by a shell reflects the grey sky and is pitted by the still falling rain and shrapnel. I keep pushing past the pool. I can see the Tommies' helmets and I head for them. I bump into bodies but they just seem to get in the way. All I can think of is getting this man back to safety. A Tommy with part of his leg missing pulls himself along. Jacky has stopped screaming which I take to be a bad sign. I roll him into the trench.

'Hold on to his head,' I yell, but my words are whipped away and no-one seems to notice. There are hands grappling with him, people impatient to get him out of the way. I turn to back down the ladder. Jacky's eyes are still fixed on me but I'm needed up here, there are too many people needing rescuing from water and the shell craters. There are people drowning up here, flailing, I can see them, I'm so close.

A few yards away a couple of our retreating soldiers kick a body into the shell pool. I carry on down the ladder. The body thrashes around and the Tommies run grinning to the waiting barbed wire and ladder. Another whiz-bang, the maroon is up.

'Hold on Jacky, I'm going out again.'

I dodge out. There's nothing but water, clouds reflected in water, pools of it chopped up by the firing, waves breaking over helmets. If only I can get a line over, keep the bloody engine going Wilf. I sway from side to side on my knees, trying to keep my balance. I see the casualty, not too far away, arms up and then disappearing under the water, I have him in my sights, Wilf take over.

The *Lucy May* rolls, I'm up at the helm, Ted throws out the lifebelt. Stormy stands by and Wilf is at my side watching the engine. Jacky, where's Jacky? And I'm out again and running and heading for the crater. He stops thrashing. Face down and floating, his uniform a sodden grey. His helmet spike sticking out of the mud a few feet away. And I'm standing for what feels like minutes but is probably no more than a blink or two and I'm in the pool, freezing, I go under, my head is under, Stella it's alright, I'll have you in a moment, hold on girl. I grab him by the hair, pull his face out of the water. Everything stops, then a gasp for air and he's trying to pull me under.

'Bitter sie, bitter sie.'

I get a foothold and pull both of us up, mud squelching in handfuls from the side of the crater. I'm slipping. It's an upturned hull of a boat that's all, I've done this so many times. I haul myself, elbows digging into the soft side, working them up. He is grabbing my leg and I pull him, my hands slipping on his drenched uniform, heaving him by his epaulets, he is kicking and spluttering and he flops onto the earth, free of the sucking mud and water.

We are breathing heavily, facing each other as if after a fight. It's quiet now. The firing has stopped. It is not Jacky and my heart lurches. The water has washed away some of the mud and his hair is a dirty blond, his eyes are blue and he has sharp cheekbones. His hand shakes, his chest is caved in and his left leg is limp. His other leg twitches uncontrollably. He flutters a swollen hand to his pocket, a ring cuts into his wedding finger.

The dogs are out now wearing white jackets with red crosses on their backs. Making low woofs they run from body to body avoiding some. They must know the life has been blown out of those. A dog heads for us. He waits patiently while I go for the brandy. All used. Water then, and trickle some onto the man's lips before taking a swig myself. His flapping hand is pulling a small leather pouch from his chest pocket; he pushes it towards me, his eyes pleading.

'Danke, danke.'

I stare at this man. I should be making him comfortable,

telling him we'll soon be back on dry land; he'll need to buy us a drink for coming out on such a foul night. But we know we would do it for anyone, on any night, any night at all. Wilf is up at helm and crossing himself like he does before any rescue and afterwards ready for the journey back and we're turning The *Lucy May* round and heading for home and the curve of lights strung out along the bay.

The lights blur, there's a dull sun and it glints off pools and the water beaded barbed wire. He comes back into focus and I look round for Wilf. There's a tug at my arm and he's there, hollow cheeks smeared with mud. Wilf pulls and hauls me back and away from this man. A dog barks next to something with only some flapping shreds of material for legs and the stretcher-bearers come running.

He lugs me down into the trench. We slide down the ladder and slip into a heap at the bottom, panting.

'What the hell do you think you were doing?' He's breathing heavily and his eyes are narrow.

'Wilf, mate,' I start. There's a smooth leather packet in my hand, it's precious somehow, its skin soft and worn with age and love. I put it to my check.

'Get rid of it you idiot,' he spits.

I shove the packet into my pocket and sink to my knees crouching against the trench wall. Sweet Crab Apple Trench. My side is searing. I fumble for a Woodbine, find a damp packet, squashed. There are a couple of usable cigarettes but I've no light and now it seems worse than any bombing, or water logged crater or legless bodies, that I can't light this fucking cigarette.

The sharp flare of sulphur. I dip my cigarette into the flame and breathe in the smoke. My heart seems to calm its relentless thumping immediately. He flicks out the match with a twist of his wrist, shakes his head and turns to walk back along the trench. His greatcoat swaying out behind him as he walks. He still manages a swagger even in these conditions. I finish my cigarette but my hand is shaking again and now I'm wondering what has just happened, what the hell has just happened?

Back in the dugout, it's sometime in the middle of the day, everything is quiet and you'd think nothing much had gone on all morning. Some of the men are shaving, dipping their razors into water in metal tins, peering into small mirrors or simply shaving with their eyes closed, feeling their way. Others polish boots and buckles. The sun is trying to come out and the rain has stopped and there is a game of cards going on. I've been asleep for a couple of hours and have woken cold and stiff and thinking about home. I roll over and feel a lump in my chest. Sitting up I pull out the leather packet and a seeping fear drips through me. I glance about, no-one is bothered about me, the card game gets louder, there's laughter. A soldier who is shaving cuts himself and swears throwing his razor into the mess can in disgust. He stems the blood with his finger. I return to the packet, a brown leather wallet, larger than a wallet. It is wet. There are receding damp patches like plaster drying out. Inside the package are tightly packed papers, the ink is smudged and has run on the first few sheets and they are stuck together and unreadable. Underneath, as I peel the layers away, the ink is clearer, letters, lists and none of them in English. A roar from the card table, one soldier stomps away. The others are laughing gathering up the cards. My heart thumps so hard they must be able to hear it. I shuffle together the sheets of paper. The card players are dealing another round; someone else has taken the first man's place. Hurriedly I shove them inside my jacket.

'Tea, Boots?' It's Wilf gazing down at me with his lazy eyes. He doesn't smile but he hands me my mug. 'What the hell were you up to earlier?' He blows on his tea. I flick my eyes towards him.

'Nothing, just bringing Jacky back.'

'Crap. After that.' He sits down, makes to light up and changes his mind.

I want to say a rescue just like we always do but I'm not quite sure what I was doing.

'And the packet? I hope you've got rid of it.' He nods towards my chest. The tea is hot for a change. I hold the mug close to my face with two hands, and the steam warms my skin. I breathe it in and it clears my head. He shrugs almost imperceptibly and at last I feel him smiling next to me.

'Present from Stella maybe?' He's teasing now.

'That's it.'

'How's she doing with that ambulance?' He takes a swig of tea; he seems to be able to drink it scalding.

'What ambulance?'

He glances at me quickly, a look of confusion passes over his eyes but only for a second.

'Didn't you say she had become an ambulance driver?'

I looked at him incredulously, 'When would she have time to drive an ambulance, she has Lily to look after?'

'Of course, I must've got it wrong, maybe she was thinking about it, or maybe I was dreaming,' he drained the mug. 'Well, you'll be home soon enough, lucky bastard.' He reaches for my mug but I shake my head, I want to hang on to the warmth for as long as possible. I need to sort out my kit bag for the journey home for a few days' rest but my mind keeps wandering to the packet next to my chest. What the hell was I thinking rescuing a bloody German? I should've let the bastard drown. And what the hell is the packet he gave me? Is it instructions of some sort? My fingers massage my chest where the lump from the packet is. I could probably be shot for this, or demoted or some damn dishonourable thing.

The card game erupts again. There's talk between a couple of soldiers in hushed voices, Harry Wright and Bill someone. I hear the word 'traitor' and try to listen in.

'Millie says the newspapers are full of it,' Harry waves his letter like a flag, the thin paper almost transparent. 'This chap was posing as an archaeologist when all the time he's spying for the Hun. Got away with it too for an age.' He folds the letter and tucks it into his pocket. 'Look out for spying traitors Millie says.'

'Should be shot.' Bill's brow is furrowed.

'Probably will be.'

I touch the lump in my jacket again. There's always talk like this. There's no need for concern. My head is thumping and I press my fingers to my temples. Stella I'll be home very soon. I'll get rid of these damn papers, no-one will ever know. But as the card game breaks up and people move about ready for the change of sentry I'm not sure exactly what it is that people will never know.

Wilfred Kay
15th September 1918
Northern France

I offered to help him with his kit bag but he shrugged me off. He's gone really miserable recently, not like the old Sam, brave, reckless some would say, pretty desperate for a bit of glory. God knows what Stella will think when she sees him, there's a change alright. He seems shrunken somehow, not the enormous plate handed, tallboy shouldered Sam, hair a bit too long. Now he's neat and trimmed and thin and caved in.

Shit, I could kick myself for mentioning the ambulance. I can't believe Stella would tell me that in one of her letters before she has told her old man.

I want to say something to him before he goes, give him something for Stella maybe but I have nothing to give. I have her letters, they'll keep me warm.

I don't know what the hell he was thinking earlier. Rescuing the damn enemy, I saw him. Sending him out again so that he can shoot more of our brothers. He could be dishonourably discharged for that I'm sure and that wallet he seems to be parading about, that wasn't a gift from Stella that's for sure. I'll be glad when he's gone and I don't have to witness any more of his stupid antics. I've a good mind to speak to the corporal, but I know I won't.

Then there's a smack on my back that knocks the stuffing out of me and Sam is beaming at my side.

'Look after the old place while I'm away Wilf.' I raise my eyes to the heavens and back but at least he's more of his old self. 'Can't hang around here.' And he's striding away, kitbag weighing him down, gas mask swinging.

'Lucky sod,' is all I can muster and I wonder at the interminable space ahead, more waiting before the next bout of madness out here. And I think about poor Jacky and wonder whether Sam did enough to save him this time.

I feel it before I hear it. Like the lifeboat maroon, I feel the thump and flare in my chest before I hear the explosion. I'm running almost before there's any sound, pulling on my helmet and skidding on the still water logged duck-boards. I get to them first, the old lifeboat callout reaction kicking in. They're a sorry sight. A scraggly little band knocked flat. Some have legs and arms at odd angles like umbrellas blown inside out, their struts broken and twisted. There's a hail of fire overhead and I try to crawl under it to reach him.

'Please God let him. . .' I don't know what I want. Let him what? What do I want? Do I want him to be breathing? Of course, he's my closest friend, my brother almost.

'Come on Sam, I'm nearly with you.'

Please God. But I can't ask for it. Images of Stella chase the pious thoughts away, Stella and Lily. I'll look after you Stella, and before I get to him I'm fantasising about how it will be if he doesn't make it.

There's a horrible mess on his head. I reach for his mouth, his neck, his chest. A shallow breath, thank God. But there's a stab of disappointment and Stella disappears from view.

The medics will be with us any minute. I reach inside his jacket for letters home in case he doesn't make it. My hand lands on the soft package, I pull it out. If it was a

German wallet I saw I can't let it be found on him. I glance round and pocket it swiftly.

'This one is still breathing, over here.' I yell to the medics and we drag him away folding his limbs back the way they're meant to go.

Wilfred Kay
17th September 1918
Northern France

'Hey Wilf, you know Jacky Prentice don't you? You know the one who went over the top by mistake like a fool.'

I glance up; the corporal is blustering as if he knows something. I won't have Jacky spoken about like that but I'm not sure I trust this strutting peacock. I give him a look, one I know usually freezes people out. He stumbles, then regains himself.

'He saw that Sam Tempest, the one you hang around with, taking a parcel from Germans.' I'm listening now alright. 'Saw it all.'

'He had half his head blown away.'

'Didn't affect his eyes though did it.' The smug bastard is parading around like a dog with a bone.

'I don't know who you're talking about.'

'Well that Sam had better look out if he comes back here, we might have something to say to him, collaborating with the Hun.'

'I don't know who you're talking about. Sam who?' I say and turn and walk away.

ELEVEN

Samuel Tempest
4th April 1919
Sussex Coast

Greatcoats were being sold at the station for a pound. They piled up in heaps as the men couldn't wait to see the back of the damned things and get the money. It's hot and they've forgotten already how useful they are in the chill. So mine is still burdening me, slung over my kitbag.

The train follows the river past chalk cuts and pulls up at the village station just before my stop. In the distance I can feel the sea and my heart quickens. It's been a long time coming this home coming. First there was the blast that sent me reeling to that military hospital in Rouen for months as they tried to put my head back together. Then, even though I was on my way home when I was hit, they decided it wasn't wise to send me home too quickly after the Armistice. By then everyone was clamouring to get back. All the bloody civil servants got back first and then those who could give people a job. I argued that I owned my own business but as I don't employ anyone I had to wait. Still, the waiting is over now and I can see the harbour and the river as the train pulls into the station. There's no-one to greet me, only because I couldn't let them know which train I would be on. It's better this way.

Lily Tempest
4th April 1919
Sussex Coast

He doesn't look like a Daddy. Not the kind I expected anyway, stern and whiskered with a newspaper and a scowl, stopping you from jumping up. He isn't like the ones who came home blinded and limping. He just stands there on the front step with a funny suit, a hat and a smile. He has a brown parcel, wrapped in string under his arm. At tea time he and Mummy burn the parcel and all its khaki-coloured contents on the fire. We hold crumpets on long forks over the flames until they are scorched and too hot to touch.

That morning the house had been full of air. I could smell it fresh and full of salt from the sea. I could smell the fishing ropes wefted with seaweed and barnacles. I was sure I even could smell France only a few miles away. On very clear days I used to run down to the lighthouse in the harbour and look as hard as I could out to sea. I screwed up my eyes and put fists to them. I peered through the openings and swore I could see Daddy standing on a French hill waving to me. There he was with a gun in one hand, his cloak neatly splayed out around him, his boots shiny like the ones on the advertisements in the news-paper.

That morning Mummy had told me to, 'go and wash to greet your Daddy who's come home from the war.' I was nervous. The only men I knew were the grocers and butchers who'd never left.

It's night time and I wake to hear a strange scuffling and some breathy cries. I call out, 'Mummy are you alright?'

I get out of bed and dance on my toes, touching the door and darting away, knowing I should not go to her but unsure why. The curtains shiver. I pull them gently apart. The river is black and lapping. I can see the railway line and the outline of a locomotive, its breathing hushed in the night. To the right and out to sea the cliffs shine like the face of the moon, opal spaces with dark ledges.

I lie awake in bed following the patterns of the curtains, watching fairies and sprites and galloping unicorns as the curtains tremble. In the morning I wake to a silence. A deep, soft silence that fills my ears and eyes and nods me off to sleep again. I drift through the rock-a-way morning until almost noon when the heat of the sun and the rattle of the train shake me to. I have a panicky I'm-late-for-school feeling, until I realise that school is a distant cloud on the horizon of the weekend with two days basking in between.

Mummy is in the kitchen making breakfast even though it's nearer lunchtime. Daddy is at the polished wooden table making bread. He turns as I come in, flour in his hair, greying his temples, Mummy's pinny wrapped around his waist, all flowers, ridiculous. He hums a tune and occasionally takes Mummy in his arms and waltzes her clumsily round the kitchen so that flour flies out around them like dust.

Daddy's bread is solid but we say it tastes wonderful.

'Daddy,' I tease, 'Mummy's feeding the birds your bread.'

'Steady there Mother,' he gasps, 'they won't be able to take off.'

We trip down to the shore past the lifeboat station, the lobster pots, the fish market and ice-house and out towards the breakwater. There where the beach falls away from the chalk cliffs sit the railway carriages, pushed in close to stop them getting washed away with the rising tides.

Samuel Tempest
10th May 1919
Sussex Coast

Lily runs down Marine Road to greet me, her dress flying. She grabs my legs and looks as if she wants swinging up but lifting her up like that makes my head thump so I come down to her level and pinch her and tickle her until she is rolling around on the ground and kicking her legs.

'There's a letter.' I stop tickling her.

'For me?' She is up now and running ahead.

'Of course for you.' And I'm running to catch her and get to the letter first. 'Can I open it?' she shouts.

'Don't open it Lily.'

'Why not? Mummy always lets me open the letters.'

'Well, Daddy doesn't,' and I have shoved past her and up the steps and through the open front door.

'Stella, where's the letter Lily is talking about?' She emerges from the kitchen

I'm breathless. 'What do you think?' She holds up some material for me to see.

'Stella, the letter, where is it?' I can feel the blood in my temples pulsating, the cut on my head throbs.

'I think she hid it.'

'What?'

'She often hides letters; it's a game we play.' Sweat starts to bead my forehead.

'For God's sake Stella.'

'Go and help her find it Sam, it's not difficult.' I put my hand to my head, 'it's just a letter that's all.'

'What did it look like?' She turns to go back to the kitchen table and her sewing.

'I didn't really see it, official looking. But it wasn't a telegram and anyway you're here so it can't be can it?' She smiles and walks away.

Shit, shit, Maybe this is it, maybe this is the letter, the summons, but what can they do now, the war is over, that packet was just letters and the rescue of a German was just a rescue. I'm really sweating now and shaking slightly.

'Lily,' my voice cracks, 'Lily, where are you love?' She sits outside at the bottom of the steps, arms round her knees. She could be crying. 'Lily, where's that letter, show Daddy where it is.' I reach out my hand and she turns away. 'Come on Lily.' I can feel the heat rise. I run my fingers around the rim of my hat, my hair sticks to my head. I can feel my voice getting angry. Stay calm, stay calm.

'Lily, where the hell is that bloody letter?' and I've lost it and I'm raging. She takes one terrified look at me and runs under my outstretched arm into the embrace of her mother who has appeared at the top of the steps.

Stella's face is black and she doesn't need to say anything. She marches inside and with a sobbing Lily and returns and shoves the letter into my trembling hand. It has a government stamp and is starched with formality. I can barely open it, the paper is flimsy, my fingers are thick and clumsy and I am sick now with the terror of being found out.

'In recognition of your conduct during the rescue of the Belgian vessel *Koning William III* on 18th August 1912, the coxswain and crew of the Lifeboat *Lady Lucille Maythorpe* will receive awards for bravery. These are to be presented on 2nd November 1919 by King Albert I of the Belgians.'

Lily Tempest
20th May 1919
Sussex Coast

Today is a special day. For my birthday, which is today, we are going on our holidays. Mummy is excited, her cheeks are pink. Daddy seems agitated. He has been quiet since the day of the letter and we are friends again now but she shakes sometimes when he talks. He snaps the suitcase closed and uses a leather belt to secure it.

'We're only going to the beach huts Sam, not to the other side of the world.' And Daddy scowls which I don't like because it's soon to be my birthday and I want everything to be perfect.

'And we don't want the contents of our lives strewn down Marine Road for all to see do we?' Daddy picks up the case and puts his hand to his head to make sure that his hat is there, which it is as always. Mummy turns, 'Are you ready Lily?' but I am already on the front steps hopping down them on one foot.

We walk to the beach. Daddy carrying the suitcase and picnic hamper. Mummy and I carry blankets and Mummy twirls her parasol. I skip along but Mummy is walking quickly and Daddy is getting left behind.

'Stella, will you slow down, anyone would think you

were desperate to see him.' Mummy shades her face with the parasol but I can see up under it and she is pink.

'Of course I want to see him, don't you? You can tell him about the awards. He'll be delighted.'

'See who Daddy?' Daddy stops and swaps the case and picnic hamper into different hands.

'Your Uncle Wilf is just back from the war.'

'Uncle Wilf, Uncle Wilf,' I am screeching and running and jumping. Mummy laughs and even Daddy smiles which makes me whoop even louder.

'You don't remember Uncle Wilf,' says Daddy, and I don't, but I am just glad to have an uncle and to be going on holiday and that it's my birthday in only a few hours time.

I run ahead and get there first. It is the afternoon and the sun bounces off the railway carriages that Mummy was calling beach huts. Light springs across the train's shiny paint work. Muslin curtains waft at windows and the doors are flung open to let in the day.

On the sand there is a large cream blanket with blue lines on it. Sitting on the blanket is a man who has dark hair and only a small smile. He shades his eyes from the sun and looks over to us as we walk towards him. He lifts his hand and waves a finger rather than his whole hand. Next to him is a polished wooden box with a handle which he starts to wind. He drops a brittle black disc into place. There is crackling and spitting, then music rings across the water. Mummy throws down her parasol and claps her hands. Daddy drops the case and the hamper and puts out his hand and pulls the man up from the sand. Uncle Wilf's leg seems to point at a funny angle at the knee, he steps towards Daddy and he has a limpy swagger. They look at each other and for a moment I think they might to cuddle. But men don't do that so they shake hands.

'Lily, this is your Uncle Wilf.' Daddy is ushering me to him to shake hands with the man and I am shy suddenly and don't know whether to curtsey or shake hands or just run away. It's my birthday soon and I don't want to feel shy. Uncle Wilf suddenly bows very low and makes a solemn arm gesture to me. He waits for me to bow as well and I am so startled that I do. Then he links my arm and says, 'May I have the honour of the first dance with the birthday girl?' and I say, 'Yes, you may.' And he puts one arm behind my back and holds my arm outstretched and before I know it he has whisked me off the ground. He swings me round in a lurching loop and we are dancing and laughing and laughing and dancing across the sand. It's alright with Uncle Wilf after that and I don't feel there are strangers at my party anymore.

Daddy wears his large white hat. His suit is white and he wears a tie even though it is hot. There is a handkerchief of the brightest blue in his top pocket. He picks daisies and pink campions and pins them onto his lapel. Mother's dress is full of flowers, little sprigs whirling around the skirt and when she dances her skirt flicks up at the edges.

Mummy only dances with Daddy even though Daddy is quite clumsy and gets his feet mixed up.

'Come on Lily, let's get these cases unpacked, then we can see if we've forgotten anything.' Daddy lifts the case and swings it up the steps of one of the carriages. There is a wooden walkway along the sides of the train like a veranda and there are striped deckchairs just waiting to be slumped in. The doors lead off this walkway and outside one there is a pair of boots. Daddy opens one of the doors and goes inside.

'We can be like the Bedouin. When they make a journey they only go a short distance for the first night so that if they've forgotten anything they can go back and get it.'

'What rubbish are you talking?' Mummy follows us up the steps.

'He's been reading too many *Boy's Own* stories,' Uncle Wilf shouts from the sand outside.

It is dark inside and it doesn't look like the carriages when the boys played in them, with glass knocked onto the floor and stuffing coming out of the seats. The seats have mostly been taken out except the long ones which lie along the carriage wall under the window. Mummy is busy making up a bed on one of these for me. There's a little partition with glass above it next to the doorway. Through the door in the partition is a big bed and through the next door there are more deckchairs and some small tables. There are little shelves with teapots and cups and a tea caddy with a black and gold pattern on it.

'We'll have to find some things to decorate the place with Lily,' Mummy shouts from the far room, 'we'll go out tomorrow and hunt.'

Outside other people have arrived.

'Lily, these are Daddy's friends from the lifeboat.'

My friend Evie has come to my party. I hold her hand and she points to her Daddy who's name is Stormy and we giggle until we are shushed up. And there is Jacky from the butcher's who doesn't hear well because he doesn't have an ear. Alfie Leburn's Dad is here and all the wives and children.

Uncle Wilf has laid out the picnic and there is birthday cake that Mummy has made especially for me. There's more dancing and singing and as it starts to get dark we look for stones that have been hollowed out by the sea. They look like skulls or the bones of birds. Uncle Wilf helps Evie and me to fill them and the scoops of shells, with wax, and we squash in some candle wicks. Then we string them in lines out to the sea. As the light fades we run about lighting them, small runways guiding us home. We build a fire on the beach and the darkness cuddles us. We sit about the fire late into the night cooking smoking potatoes. We poke them with sticks until they are burnt and crisp on the outside, and steaming and fluffy beneath the crust.

Evie and I curl up together in blankets and listen as Mummy talks about the dive show she used to run and I think of her diving like a swallow deep into the swirling blue in front of a gasping crowd. I see her bobbing up like a seal, basking in adoration, before she swims elegantly back and climbs out, dripping and shiny, to rapturous applause.

She talks of how she met Daddy, the day he rescued her from the sea. I think of Daddy ripping off his jacket and clambering onto the railings and hurling himself into the churning broth beneath. I think of how brave he is. His face glows in the firelight. He jokes saying Uncle Wilf wanted to jump in but couldn't swim until Mummy kicks him. Uncle Wilf sits further back lying on one elbow, in his other hand burns a cigarette. His face in shadow.

'Come on,' says Mummy, 'it must be time for bed for these girls,' but Daddy stops her with a hand on her arm.

'There may not be another tomorrow,' he says, and I burrow into the blankets on the sand until I fall asleep and am carried, curled like an animal, into the railway carriage. At night I dream of Mummy as a seal woman, sleek and silky dipping between the waves.

TWELVE

Samuel Tempest
2nd June 1919
Sussex Coast

I walk in the morning before even Lily has woken and sit on the beach. I make myself watch the mist rise even though I can hardly bare it. The mist swirls across the bay, it pushes on. I know it is mist. I know it will not reach me. The sun burns it off before it gets this far inland. But just when I can stand it no longer and I can see his flailing arms, his yellow blond hair, saturated and dripping, the lighthouse comes into view and hovers above the eddies. The sun breaks through and I am myself again or the person I have become.

After I received the letter I was relieved but then the worry that it is only a matter of time until I'm found out started growing again. So I wait. Apparently I've been counting the boys back in over the last few months. Stella tells me off about it but what does she know, she wasn't there. Jacky is back, hard of hearing, but that's not much for what he's been through. I've been checking on him though making sure he's safe, but when I look at him I see how grateful he is to me. I think that's a thing I've wanted all my life, for people to be grateful, and now it sickens me. And Wilf of course. I think I'm glad Wilf is back but Ted hasn't returned and no-one is sure whether he is alive or dead. We have lost our navigator and it feels as if we've lost our way. Jacky will step into his shoes but it all feels too soon, it's still too soon. I keep thinking that if only I had been there, I would have been able to do something. But Stormy is back, he was back first with his 'Blighty wound' but we're not sure if he'll be able to serve on The *Lucy May* again. Jerry is fine, of course he never went anywhere in the first place, over forty-one, lucky bastard. I wish we'd all been old codgers. And then there is Ted. I know I could have saved Ted, if only they hadn't split us up, if I could have had some control over them, they're my crew, but no . . . and on and on I go, over and over it all again and again. Like some horrible moving picture stuttering across the screen in my head.

I want to join in the antics at the carriages but after that first day I have struggled to. I feel drawn to the workshop, to my own company or to the company of those who were there. Everyone else will make some inane comments, even Stella – in fact, especially Stella. Buck up, it's over now, look at you, you're fine, that scar will heal and you'll be the same old Sam again, stiff upper lip, it's all behind you. It's all behind me and in front of me and all around me, that's the trouble. So I leave them to it. They don't seem to need me anyway. Stella and Wilf are like a couple of schoolchildren playing with Lily. So Wilf can't help and I'm still weary of him. He feels predatory as if he's waiting to pounce, to disclose something and ruin me. So I stick to myself.

I keep replaying it, my time in France, sounds like a holiday doesn't it? Except that it was no holiday. Over and over my memory stutters and starts, sometimes clear as if I am back there, sometimes fitfully as if I am watching someone else. I don't often recall the horror of it, usually it is the monotony, the routine, the trudging boredom of it that haunts me. At night I can recall a whole route march, I'll lie awake rapt by each footfall. Sometimes while working at the workshop I start turning it over and over. Why did I rush into the water-drenched shell-hole to rescue the German? I watch the rain run down his face like tears. I wonder about the package, if there was a package. I find it hard to remember some-times. I think he handed me a package and I passed it on. I didn't have it when I reached the hospital so who did I pass it to? Or maybe it was found on me and if it was it's only a matter of time, even now, before they come and get me. And I worry about what Wilf saw. So I am wary of him and watchful. I think he saw me save the life of a German soldier and if he did does he hold it against me? Of course he does, I should have been saving our boys and instead I blunder about saving the bloody enemy. The question is when will he choose to let me know what he has seen? In front of Stella? In front of the King? That's it, in front of the King of Belgium and the whole damn town. And then the wind startles me and I realise that, of course, this is all rubbish but if I think about the package pressed into my hand I become confused and so it's better to concentrate on ordinary things.

I can pick out all the landmarks on our marches; I seem to be able to recall some things, irrelevant things, in amazing detail and accuracy. Other things I cannot remember at all. If one of the boys talks about something that happened to us, Jacky perhaps, I might have no recollection and find it hard to believe that I was there. I should ask Wilf if he feels the same but he seems to have grown somehow despite his experiences. His only wound is the one he sustained at sea before we even went to war and that seems only to have added to his personality. Now he has a swagger and it makes him look heroic. That's a real injury. Not like the one I have that refuses to heal, that no-one can see because if they did they would flinch from it in horror. So I hide it and then no-one knows it's there. I'm just a strange man who always wears a hat and who refuses to take it off even inside, even when women come into the room. So instead of looking courageous, at best I look eccentric and at worst rude and cantankerous. Wilf would probably carry it off better than me; he'd probably make it look mysterious. He seems so damned unaffected by it all and I wonder if that's what prayer does, make you strong, or make you forget or make you able to bare it.

So I concentrate on the small things, things where I can make a difference. Counting shells on my morning walks

I wonder if you count the shells whether every seventh one would be the biggest. Just like counting waves. They fall into patterns of large and small, if you are patient you can see shapes in the rise and fall. How many times have I stood, counting and counting? If you get the timing wrong a wave will crash a boat back onto the beach. And I run through the names, Sullivan, Dempster, Edwards, Smith, Ted and Stan. I count and recount the people that were killed in a day to see if there were patterns, I watch the sky traced out bullets.

THIRTEEN

Stella Maris
10th June 1919
Sussex Coast

'I'm not going to say, where the hell have you been? Or, what in God's name have you been doing all this time? Or, why are you never here, or even, why don't you play with Lily.' I'm in full stride now and, despite Lily being curled asleep behind the partition, I am banging pans and cutlery in an attempt to put them onto a shelf.

'I'm not even going to ask whether you would prefer us to be at home rather than here at the carriages, because quite honestly I'd rather be here where there are things to take my mind off the fact that you are never with us.' I have a tin cup in my hand and I am gripping the handle so hard I am glad it is tin and not china.

'Sam, we've been alone so long.' He is stood on the veranda. The door is open but he is wavering on the threshold, not sure whether to come into the heart of my rage or stay outside in the still night air.

'You'll wake Lily.' I say to him completely foolishly because the only person likely to wake Lily is me and I have probably already done so. He runs his hand through the hair at his temple and looks distracted. He moves the hat as if letting off steam and I catch a glimpse of the still raw looking scar which ravishes the side of his head. As he lifts his arm there is a line of dust along his shirt sleeve. It looks as if he has fallen asleep on his workbench with his head on an arm strewn through the wood shavings. So now it seems as if he would rather sleep uncomfortably at his work than lie next to me.

So I dare not ask if he would rather be alone in his workshop than here with us because I'm afraid of the answer. I put the cup I am holding down heavily on the table and pour him some whisky. Instead of passing it to him I put the cup to my own lips and the liquid burns over my tongue and slides down my throat a little too well. I pour some more and hand it to him. It's a kind of peace offering. My version of a white flag. He takes it and steps over the threshold. Why doesn't he say anything? Why doesn't he rage and rail and scream at me? Why does he just drink and look as if he'd rather be anywhere than here.

'I don't think you need me,' he says, and looks at the floor of the carriage.

'What do you mean? I don't need you, why do you need to be needed? Why do I have to need you? I want you. I'm with you. Why do I have to need you as well? You seem to forget that I was a woman of independent means before I met you, why would I need a man?' And I realise that that is it. That's the problem. All along Sam has wanted, expected, to be needed by everyone, his customers, his lifeboat crew, by those he rescues and, he thought, by me.

'Sam, I needed you in the water, when you rescued me, I needed you then.' His eyes flicker toward me and then away.

'But you haven't needed me since.'

'I gave up my dive show didn't I? Isn't that a kind of need?' He doesn't answer. 'Sam, it was a huge thing for me. I never thought I'd do that for anyone.' He drains the last of the whiskey. 'People do need you.'

'I don't know who, they all know Wilf could coxswain The *Lucy May* and probably do a better job of it than me. He's practically been doing it for years anyway, I'm just a figure head.'

'What?'

'And there's no money in boat building, no-one's interested anymore.'

'That's only because people are too busy trying to rebuild their lives Sam. That won't last and you need to be there for them when they come back. Anyway you have orders haven't you?' But he isn't listening; he's turned to the sea, the pull and the rush of it.

'Even Lily needs you more than me,' he says.

I'm about to say this is ridiculous and of course a child needs her mother and that he hasn't been here for most of her life so what does he expect but he has walked away down the steps of the carriage.

'Sam.'

'I'm just going to have a smoke.'

And so Sam, who hates cigarettes and smoking, walks towards the cliffs; he sits upon a rock, the light from his cigarette intermittently flashing as he moves, sending out its SOS out into the night.

Lily Tempest
15th June 1919
Sussex Coast

I've been dreaming of playing hide and seek around the carriages then something woke me but I can still remember my dream. We played inside this afternoon because the wind had been getting up and there was a storm on the way and Mummy and Uncle Wilf thought it better that we stayed inside. I didn't think the wind seemed too bad but I love hide and seek. I hid in some really good places, and Mummy and Uncle Wilf couldn't find me for ages. I slid under one of the seats and pulled Mummy's shawl which was on the seat down, so it covered the gap and there I lay quietly breathing. I nearly gave myself away so many times when they came close, and once Mummy even rustled her shawl but she didn't spot me and I put my hand in my mouth to stop myself giggling or shouting out, 'Here I am.'

I wonder if the thing that woke me just now was Daddy coming back from work or just the wind dragging at the carriages and pulling me out of my sleep.

Outside it's dark. The beam from the lighthouse swings

across the bay every few seconds, like a searchlight, it lights up the water. I kneel up and press my nose to the window and feel its cool skin against mine. There's no sound at all from the carriage. I tiptoe across the floor and peep through the glass partition that separates my part of the carriage from Mummy and Daddy's. The bed is made and there are no sleeping lumps in it. My heart starts pounding loudly because they must have run away and left me and I could pinch myself for going to sleep in the first place. If I'd stayed awake they never would have been able to get to the door. I would have got there first and stopped them leaving me. A noise from outside and I'm back at the window again, cupping my hands round my face against the glass. There is a flash of material and the fringe of Mummy's shawl. I can just make her out to the right. She's on the veranda and my heart slows. Surely if she were running away she would have more than just a shawl and now she is taking off her shoes so she really can't be running far and I am about to lie down again when I hear the door next to ours creak and then there are some muffled sounds. Mummy's voice and then a deeper one that must be Daddy's. They must be visiting Uncle Wilf to play cards, or drink whisky.

The sea grinds over the pebbles and sucks at them leaving them wet and shining in the moonlight. Next door there are little noises, squeaks and a clatter as something heavy falls to the floor. The carriage begins to tremble and rock. The wind has been getting stronger all night, it bites at the chains of boats and smacks the sails, a gust whips the side of the carriage and it shudders.

Stella Maris
16th June 1919
Sussex Coast

'Come on Lily, let's get packed. We're going home this morning.' I push clothes and crockery into the suitcase and wonder how on earth we managed to fit everything in. There have been several trips home in between to pick up more essentials and now there seems to be no chance of all our possessions fitting. But I do not want to make two journeys, so I squash plates and cups and stockings and dresses in any old how.

'Why are we going home?' Lily is sleepy and has her bucketful of sea shells in her hand, in case we forget it.

'Look outside Lily, it isn't beach weather. Didn't you hear the storm?'

'I heard something.' She kneels on a carriage seat to see out of the window. The beach is strewn with tangled fishing nets, bits of packing crate and old railway sleepers. Seaweed lies rotting in heaps and pages of a newspaper flutter like an injured bird caught in the debris.

I need to get away. Going home won't help but if I stay here any longer I know I will never go home. So I pack and chatter to Lily. I quickly roll my hair into a knot at the back, fastening it with a few pins, when I see him on the veranda. I duck instinctively although there's nothing to hide behind. So I turn away from the window. Like a child playing hide-and-seek and hiding their eyes thinking it makes them invisible. If I can't see him; he can't see me. If I look into his eyes I won't be able to leave and for Lily's sake I must. I sneak a look while still facing the other way. He is not looking towards my window, instead he views the devastation on the beach. He takes a packet from his pocket, opens it and taps a cigarette on the box before putting it into his mouth. If he sits on the veranda he will block our escape and I feel suddenly flushed and flustered. Then Lily solves my dilemma by spotting him and flying from the carriage. She throws her arm around his neck and knocks her bucket against his back, spilling some shells.

'Steady there ship mate,' he says and pulls her round onto his lap to look at the beach.

Wilf insists on carrying the bags. He can't say anything with Lily there but I can see the drained look on his face

99

when he realises we are leaving. Lily skips along twittering to us both while Wilf carries both case and hamper, stuffed to the brim with our passions, to the start of Marine Road where I take them from him in case we're seen. Lily grasps one of the handles of the picnic hamper and we roll up the road, our different heights and strengths making us lurch with our burden. I cannot look back but I can feel his eyes staring after us all the way. The road is strewn with the chaos of the night before, a child's doll bereft of clothes which Lily wants to take home but I won't let her, a woman's shoe, just one shoe, a book with its pages ruffled and its spine broken.

And then the weight of the case is too much. I have forgotten the belt I mocked Sam for having all those weeks ago and the catches are weak and without Sam's strong strapping the case threatens to spring loose and spread our lives across the public highway. I drop the case and sit down heavily upon it, my head in my hands. It is too much, the weight of it all, the case, the war, Sam's rejection, the impossibility of Wilf. All I can feel are his arms engulfing me, his fingers in my mouth, salty with sweat, His skin surprisingly smooth and soft when I pressed him to me. The tight muscles beneath. My fingers tracing every one of his ribs. His stomach hard like the ridges left in sand when the tide rushes out.

FOURTEEN

Lily Tempest
24th June 1919
Sussex Coast

Thunder growls out of the sky but we are going to the boating lake anyway. It's alright because it's only the giants moving their furniture around. It sounds like mountain tigers on the prowl to me. There's a really loud clatter.

'That's Daddy giant dropping the wardrobe down the stairs.' Mummy is carrying the yacht because my stockings keep itching and I have to keep stopping to scratch my legs. I carry the stick Daddy has made to push the boat – it's also good for warding off mountain tigers, thrashing grass and itching the backs of my knees. I wonder about the giants' wardrobe. I want to ask why they need their wardrobe downstairs anyway but we are at the lake and Mummy is settling my boat down on a bald piece of grass next to the water's edge. It tips over onto its keel, all leaned over as if racing in really windy weather.

Mummy is quiet, thinking big adult thoughts. She gazes back the way we've come. She stands with her back to the water. She seems to be looking at me but when I look up she is staring over my shoulder.

'So Lily, are you going to name your boat on her maiden voyage?' she says. She sounds excited and her cheeks are pink but she still isn't really looking at me.

I pick up the boat. It has a shining wooden hull which Daddy has sanded and polished until I can make faces in it. Her sails are creamy white. There's a space left for her name to be painted on. I stand at the edge of the water, the lip of the land lapping the toes of my shoes.

'Daddy should be here for her first sail, it isn't right without him.'

'Your father's busy.' It seemed that he was always busy. I thought now he'd finished my boat we'd see him more.

The thunder groans on and Mummy looks at me and smiles.

'Come on before it rains.' She is suddenly busy helping me to lower the boat, lifting up her skirt and tucking it under her knees as she crouches down to my height. The sky is the colour of train smoke. Big fat juicy drops of rain bounce onto the deck of the boat.

'Do you know what you're calling her?'

'I name this ship,' I shout and I stand up for the occasion and Mummy stands too holding her skirt in one hand, "*The Martlet*," and we both salute.

'Are you going to fly away in her?' Mummy says. *The Martlet* bobs uncertainly in the water.

'Daddy wants to fly away.' A gust of wind bends the tree branches and rocks the boat. I push her bow with the stick. The rain is harder now. Mummy turns suddenly, dropping the hem of her white skirt. It trails in the mud next to the pond but she doesn't seem to notice. I turn as well and there he is standing facing Mummy.

'Uncle Wilf,' I yell, 'look at *The Martlet*, she's finished.' I'm really happy now because you need more than two people for a boat launch and three is nearly a crowd.' I take his hand and he stumbles a little towards the boat. I tell him how beautiful she is and how long it took Daddy to make her.

'Watch how she goes,' and I jab her with the stick.

'She's beautiful,' he says still looking at Mummy, 'so graceful. A beautiful mythological bird.' Mummy smiles, 'I've never seen such a beautiful creation,' and I'm pleased and push the boat further round the edge of the pond.

'Look at her,' I cry.

'She has lovely lines,' he says and Mummy giggles and looks away.

'She goes like the wind,' I'm screaming now and running and pushing the boat on.

'I know,' he says and Mummy gives him a little punch on the arm and they walk on behind me.

The rain falls heavier now and my dress has dark patches on it. I run too far ahead and only catch bits of Mummy and Uncle Wilf's conversation.

'Well?' they are walking very close, almost touching.

'You can't tell him.'

'Don't you want me to?' she looks at Uncle Wilf and stops still.

'Of course,' he says. 'It's wrong Stella, what we're doing.'

'Why is it wrong?'

'Haven't you heard of the Ten Commandments?'

'I don't care about the Ten Commandments.'

'Thou shalt not commit adultery. It's the seventh Commandment. It comes before thou shalt not steal.'

'I'm not married, so we're not committing adultery.' He looks at her strangely. 'Although technically it might come under the stealing one if you want to be pedantic.'

'Stella.'

'We're not hurting anyone Wilf.'

'Except ourselves.'

'Does saying it's wrong somehow makes it better?' Mummy pulls herself away from him but she still holds his hands. 'Does it cleanse your good Catholic soul? Bring you somewhere closer to absolution?'

The rain runs down his back and he shakes himself like a dog and the water flies out. Mummy closes her eyes, water runs down her face like tears. Then he says 'No . . . I don't know. Maybe. Come away with me, both of you.'

'Where are we going Uncle Wilf?' and I'm back at them and jumping up. He lets go of Mummy's hand and lifts me high in the air and makes me fly.

'Where do you want to go? Where shall we go? Away, far away,' and he swings me round and round. 'How about elephant stalking,' he yells.

'Or tiger tracking,' I shriek.

The rain flies out of my hair as I swing and Mummy smoothes her sodden dress. And then a fizz that sounds like giant sherbets and I know the crack is coming and I'm down with a jolt in the mud and he is running. He turns still skipping backwards and looks at Mummy and then he is gone through the park gates and off towards the lifeboat station. *The Martlet* skims away. I wave my stick and lean out over the water but she drifts out of reach. Mummy rubs her hands through her wringing hair; her white dress, heavy and laden with water, sticks in dark patches to her body.

Wilfred Kay
24th June 1919
Sussex Coast

I run. I'm too close to the jetty to get Ophelia and I'm pretty fast anyway even with my gammy leg. I'm at the hut first. I can see Jacky moving through the red sea of the fish market. The workers part swiftly to let him through. Sam should be here but I can't see him. The doors to his workshop are open and gaping which is strange because even when he leaves in a hurry he manages to lock them.

The second maroon is up, but I'm there already and pushing through the small crowd that's gathered. I try to press the thoughts of Stella out of my mind. Stella with her hair in wet ringlets, Stella with her dress clinging to her curves. Stella.

Jerry isn't waiting with the life vests so I go to grab them from the lifeboat house. It's then that I see Sam. He is crouched under the table. The whisky bottle and an unfinished game of blackjack still scattered over it. His arms shroud his head and his hands grip the table leg, his knuckles are white like they are when he's riding in Ophelia. Except this is no joy ride. He is shaking and rocking the table hard, making it judder.

There's a hurried footstep at the door and Jacky stands panting and holding his side.

'Make The *Lucy May* ready,' I mouth at him, 'Sam's not coming with us.' I accentuate the words to make up for his hearing loss and I try to shield the view of Sam. It's useless. My frame won't fill the doorway like Sam's would have and Jacky sees the wrecked man who is waiting for the next bomb blast or round of shrapnel.

'Bloody maroons,' Jacky says, 'it's alright for me, I can barely bloody hear them,' and he touches the place where his ear should be. 'If it wasn't for the lads in the shop pushing me out the door I'd never be here.' He looks guiltily at his hands still covered in blood from chopping meat.

'Don't let him see you while he is like that and don't tell them, Jacky,' but I need not have said it. The look on Jacky's face tells me he would walk through fire for this man.

The crew all seem to arrive together suddenly and Jacky has the kit off me and is handing it round, ushering and clucking like a mother hen gathering his brood onto the boat, making ready, focused, proud, in control.

I touch Sam's head and he jerks toward me but his face is a blank and his mouth hangs limp. He seems to recognise me for a moment and then he ducks an imaginary bullet and is back at the front. Lost to me. I lock him in so no-one can find him. What else can I do? I throw the key through the window and hope that when he comes through it he can release himself from his prison.

I leap onto The *Lucy May* as Jerry knocks out the holding pins and we crash into the churning waves.

Wilfred Kay
25th June 1919
Sussex Coast

So Sam is lost to me. He is shrunken in his own body. Our first lifeboat rescue without him and we brought the vessel in without injury or man overboard or incident. I wondered if the crew missed their usual enforced excitement. If they would spurn my methodical manner but it seems we have all had too much excitement for one lifetime. And we have two new members now training up to step in where Ted and Stan left off. Jacky seems to have grown somehow, he didn't want to let Sam down. He was a model lifeboat man, calm, in control, showing us the way. He'll make a great coxswain one day.

As the crew grow Sam shrinks. He tries to make up some story about why he wasn't there but he finds it hard to catch anyone's eye anymore, especially mine. He knows I saw him like that, so different from seeing him torn and cracked from the explosion. That was an honourable, acceptable injury. This is different and it's knocked the stuffing out of him well and truly. It isn't that Sam's courage has left him, it's more that it was never courage in the first place. He just didn't realise it and the shattering of his illusion is what is breaking him. The knowledge that he can't do it alone, that he has never been able to. Perhaps he is also worried about that stupid rescue in the trenches and the letters he had. I mean to tell him that I have the packet, it was me who took it from him and it's alright so I stop by his workshop today. As ever he is concentrating on fiddly little bits of wood, piecing together another toy yacht.

I lean on the door jamb, 'I thought you'd finished Lily's boat.' Sam's eyes flicker towards me but he doesn't stop what he's doing. 'She's had her maiden voyage, she goes beautifully.'

'I can always do better,' he bends and looks along the curve of wood, 'it wasn't good enough for her, she deserves better. This one will be better.'

'What about the orders Sam?' I eye the dusty order books and paperwork jumbled on Sam's makeshift office desk in the corner. He never was one for paperwork but this hadn't been touched for weeks.

His eyes wander around the workshop and back to his toy.

'I'm coming to them; this is what's important at the moment.'

'She has to eat Sam, and Stella, and you for that matter.' His shirt hangs off his shoulders and I wonder at the job Stella must be having trying to get him to take food.

I have not mentioned the packet and do not know how to. Later I wonder whether it is because I have some kind of power over him and I hate myself.

He starts planning, it becomes manic, he leans so hard the wood cracks. He curses and throws it to the floor. He reaches for another, a beautiful piece of oak too large to cut down for a child's toy.

'Sam not that piece surely,' but already he is sawing into it.

Samuel Tempest
27th June 1919
Sussex Coast

I leave the workshop and walk out to the beach. The door stands open and flapping but it doesn't seem to matter, what matters at this moment in time is finding a shell to decorate Lily's boat or maybe just to take back to her tonight. There's a buzzing in my head and I can't shake the memory of this morning when Lily flew at me from the stairs and wanted swinging round. The house is too small so she dragged me to the garden but the buzzing became unbearable and I couldn't lift her and something snapped and she ran inside crying that I never played with her and that Uncle Wilf would have swung her. There he is again, perfect Uncle Wilf, perfect, perfect. I can't shake the thought of him swinging Lily. The thought of him seeing me crumpled, of rescuing me, of seeing me rescue the bloody German, of taking my crew on a callout. So I left the workshop thinking a shell would be the thing to take Lily's mind off perfect Uncle Wilf. She has quite a collection and a shell chosen by her Daddy especially for her would be the thing to make her smile at me again.

The beach squeaks as I walk. Sun is trying to spill through the mist. One of the posts holding the breakwater is seat height and just right for sitting and sorting through shells and pebble and stone. I push my hand into the scrunchy mix and let it fall through my fingers, it looks just like a quarter of lemon drops and mint imperials that Lily might shovel out at the corner shop.

It seems to be the small things that interest me now, things in miniature: Lily's boats, the sand on the beach, the swirl of a shell. I have seen spirals in shells, on staircases, in the thread that connects the barrel of a gun to its shaft. Increasingly now I wonder at the beauty of a spiral and think of the repeating shapes I have seen. Sometimes it feels as if I see everything in shapes and patterns. The stains on a dishcloth, the burn marks on a wooden table, the ragged edge of the coast which smoothes then becomes jagged again. Even a tap dripping, irregular and out of time, soon seems to fall into a pattern. After a while the drips waver and then form themselves into a new rhythm. When marching, even the raggiest of recruits falls into a rhythm. The soldier marching, half asleep with exhaustion, stumbles but falls into a new time. Could this have been predicted? Wilf would believe it was God who made these things and caused them to fall into patterns, but for me the answers are not so convenient.

I pick up a whelk shell, a perfect thing with no fracture. The lines radiate out like sunrays. The spiral twists onto its perfect tail, like the soft folds of an ear. Like Jacky's ear. And I drop the shell, the raging animal in my stomach threatening to erupt.

Stella Maris
3rd October 1919
Sussex Coast

I fill my days as best I can, there's only so much cleaning and washing you can do and for me I usually only clean properly when the boys are on a callout. But I live for the hour in the middle of the day. The hour when Wilf is here. Just one little hour a day. Not much but it is everything. I left the carriages to get away from him to save me from myself really but he followed me here and I am glad. Lily is at school and we have become reckless. Sam has taken to having lunch at the workshop, I go down at eleven with some food, I used to cook something especially but he never seemed to eat it so now I take bread and cheese but he usually returns at night with it uneaten. At first this worried me but now he seems to be disappearing to me, wasting away physically and in my mind. I can't focus on him the same way and my head is so full of Wilf that I cannot find time to worry about Sam not eating and then I am guilty and start worrying all over again.

I cannot see my dreams. I cannot remember them afterwards but it seems they are vivid. Sam recalls them for me when he is feeling lucid and able. They invade his sleep. And my thrashing and talking has left me open. I feel him draw away from me in the mornings. And then my head fills up with thoughts of Wilf once again and I cannot worry.

Wilf used to eat his lunch with the boys from the railway or more often than not sit in Ophelia to get some peace. Now he arrives at the back door, his breath heavy from running but he leans against the door jamb as if he has all the time in the world. I have taken to looking for him, watching the tide rise and fall. I say I don't watch but I find things to busy myself with in Lily's room which overlooks the garden and railway line, hoping to see him come running. I watch him straighten his jacket and smooth his hair which sticks up at the front no matter what he does with it. He has engine oil under his finger nails. I hear him scrubbing them in the butt of rain water in the garden. When I go to the door his hands are damp, he runs them through his hair nervously and the water glistens there at his temples.

Stella Maris
4th October 1919
Sussex Coast

I hear the latch on the back door and my heart ricochets off my ribs. The feeling is so violent I hold on to the back of a chair for a moment but it is late in the afternoon and Wilf was here only a few hours ago. I cannot be him again. When I see Sam's blond head I try to look pleased just as he tries to look pleased to see me.

'There's a letter for you?' I take his coat and in so doing I brush his hand. It is really cold. The nights are drawing in and the air feels ready to snap. I hang his coat on a peg in the hall and when I come back I expect him to be opening the letter.

'It's on the mantelpiece,' tucked just behind the sloping sides of the clock but really obvious. It's the finest letter I have ever seen and something in me swells just to see it there on our mantelpiece. I'm jumping inside wanting him to open it.

He studies it with his arms close to his body as if afraid to touch it. He leans forward as if he's looking at a painting on the wall of a fancy house, not daring to touch.

'Sam, open it, I can't wait any longer. It's been winking at me all day saying, "open me, open me." I've nearly opened it a hundred times.' He steps back away from the mantelpiece. Below it I have laid the fire ready. It is getting chilly and I want him to light it.

'It has the royal insignia look, on the wax seal.' I pick up the letter, it is heavy and thick and I turn it over to show him the burgundy embossed seal.

'Why don't you open it,' he says. 'We know what it says anyway.' He turns and walks to the kitchen pushing up the sleeves of his shirt. He turns on the tap and washes his hands and arms up the elbow, rubbing hard with the block of soap.

'Alright, well, I will open it then.' And I carefully pull apart the seal trying to keep as much of it in place as possible. I take out the thick cream card inside and read.

'It's from the King of Belgium; he invites you to a ceremony recognising the rescue of the vessel *Koning William III*. He wants to present you and the crew with awards for your bravery. That's great news Sam.'

Sam coughs.

'Well? It's not every day that you get a letter from a King.' I'm skipping around the room like Lily.

'Be careful Stella.'

'Careful of what? I've a letter from a king, why do I need to be careful?' And I hug it to me. 'Do you think the Queen will come, is there a Queen? What on earth will we wear?'

Sam stands with his hands gripping the edge of the sink. I can see the whites of his knuckles and he is staring down into the suds.

'I'm not going.' He said it quietly but it stops me dancing and although the letter had warmed me for a while now I feel the chill of the room.

'What do you mean you're not going, you don't even know when it is?'

'It doesn't matter when it is.'

'But it will be wonderful for the crew.'

'Well they can go; they deserve it, they should go.'

'You deserve it.'

He turns and stares at me as if this is the most ridiculous thing I could have said. I can't be bothered to argue. I stuff the card back into its envelope and stand it back on the mantelpiece. I think of Wilf and his quiet delight at receiving an award for bravery. He'll pretend he isn't but secretly he will be thrilled. Perhaps if Sam isn't there all the better for Wilf, at least he won't be upstaged by Sam as usual. I light the fire quickly, too quickly, it goes out, and I curse. I try again and hear the back door open and close again and he has gone out, without his jacket, into the darkness.

FIFTEEN

Lily Tempest
1st November 1919
Sussex Coast

The front door closes softly. But I'm awake and up and leaning my elbows on the windowsill to peer out of the frosted pane. I wrap the rosebud curtains around my body and tuck my hands under my arms for warmth. A sharp draught flies from the window and I have to keep rubbing the glass because it mists up. What if I hold my breath? That's better, now I can see. Then I let it out in one large huff and the view glazes over again. I shuffle from foot to foot. The sky outside is brightening.

Daddy is in the back garden wearing his white hat as ever. It glistens like frost. His long greatcoat sweeps his legs. He is turned to the side, his head held at an angle as if he is listening. He looks sort of slept in, like you'd look if you were a bed that someone had tossed and turned in all night. He's whispering and I strain to hear, pushing myself closer to the pane until I almost become part of the freezing glass. He's talking to someone who is standing at the kitchen door. It must be Mummy although I cannot see her. I can tell they're arguing even though they are whispering. A whisper can cut as loud as any shout when it is hurled in an argument.

'Please don't go back, Daddy,' I mouth through the window, 'please don't leave us again.'

He doesn't look as if he's leaving. There's no khaki bag slung over his shoulder, no uniform. Besides he had said months ago, while jumping me over fences at the gymkhana on his knee, that he was never going back and they'd have to shoot him first. I remembered that. I shuffle my feet again on the cold floor, stepping them up inside my nightdress for warmth. Perhaps that was it; perhaps he was going to be shot. You wouldn't need much to be shot would you? Maybe that's why they were arguing. Perhaps he's saying he won't go back and Mummy is afraid he will be shot. But the war is over, everyone knows that. I blow on my hands, the air from my breath warming them for a moment. I'm shivering properly now, either from the cold or from fear or from excitement. I press my ear to the glass.

'I'm not going,' he says, and I breathe a happy sigh.

Mummy is speaking now, she says, 'You have to go, what on earth will everyone think?'

'I don't damn well care what anyone thinks. I'm not worthy of it.'

'What do you mean you're not worthy? You were there, I've heard what they said, you were as brave as the next man. In fact you were the one who saved the Captain's wife and child, it was you Sam.'

Daddy mutters something I can't hear and stares at Mummy defiantly.

'What, so you're saying you're a coward now?' Her voice has crept above a whisper.

'Better to be a coward and stick to what you believe in,' he spits.

'I won't have my husband called a coward.'

'So you'd rather just know he was would you?'

'I'd rather he proudly accepted his award for bravery. An award he deserves.'

'I wasn't brave.' He is stamping his feet now and slapping his arms against his sides. Great puffs of smoky air escape from his mouth. 'I'm never brave. I was just part of a crew. Leave me to my own devices and you don't know what I might do.'

I can't hear Mummy's answer. The early train rumbles past and Daddy's next comment is whipped away by the carriages.

At least he isn't going away. I suppose he's decided not to go to the award ceremony, that much is clear. I'm still not sure about him being shot though. They shoot cowards don't they? He walks out of the gate at the bottom of the garden and crosses the railway track heading towards his workshop, collar turned up against the cold.

SIXTEEN

Wilfred Kay
2nd November 1919
Sussex Coast

The town is full of ribbons and banners: red, white and
blue. Another patriotic excuse for a knees-up to mark the
end of the war. There isn't much wind so the flags hang
limply and shiver on their masts.

I have been feeling sick for a couple of days and I can't
work out if it's the impending ceremony and the thought
of all those faces peering at me, or the worry that Sam
might do something stupid or just the thought of Stella.
The thought of her has been growing in my chest. She fills
me up and consumes most of my waking thought.

Driving Ophelia through the streets is a tricky business,
avoiding horses and carts. People run with last-minute
chairs towards the recreation ground. Others button their
coats against the cold and look to the ground and they
hurry along, stepping out in front of the car. I hoot and
those that don't know me look scornfully at Ophelia.
Where Marine Road crosses the High Street I have the
usual indecision. It's a good job Sam isn't in the car. When
he is here he always wants me to slow down at crossroads
and hoot a lot. All I want to do is drive really fast to get
across. It's strange how he could be so reckless at sea and
so full of fear on land. He isn't here so I drive quickly. I
slow down when I get to Jacky's Butchery to avoid the old
red setter lying in the road outside, his coat full of
sawdust from the shop floor. He hides his nose under a
paw to keep warm. Jacky is inside up to his eyes in it and
I shout at him to get a move on. He doesn't hear me of
course and I leap from the car leaving her engine running.

The dog moves lazily to see what the commotion is all about as I jump over him and into the shop doorway.

'Jacky, come on mate, you'll be late, get cleaned up.'

He sees me in the doorway, my arms stretched up the wooden frame, foot tapping, agitated. He wipes his hand across his face, leaving a smear of blood, and shrugs in a helpless manner.

'Come on boys, get him cleaned up and out of here,' and the young apprentice appears from the back room to take over. My heart is thumping as if we've been called out on a shout as I get back into Ophelia and lurch off down the road waving and hooting and just missing the town band who are kitted out and gathering for a final rehearsal.

I head to Sam's workshop, trying to catch him alone. I assume he might be mooching around there. I pull up outside and check the package inside my pocket, it's warm and soft and densely packed.

'Sam, mate.' I call to the door of the shed. It stands ajar, he must be inside. 'Look, I've been meaning to give you this back for ages but, well, you know how it is.' Inside something stirs, 'Sam, it's only a load of love letters mate, nothing sinister,' and I heave open the door, a couple of pigeons fly up, grey, they fly out past me, their wings clacking. He is not in the workshop and I begin to feel guilty about the package, for holding onto it for so long. He must have known it was only love letters, surely he wouldn't think they were anything else, but as I close the doors and drive away I wonder whether the burden of the parcel has weighed on him too much.

On Marine Road I pull up outside Sam and Stella's. There's no sign of them. I still can't quite believe that he won't come to the ceremony knowing Sam's thirst for some kind of adoration but he's been adamant for weeks that that he won't be there. If he isn't it will leave me in his shoes to head up the crew. The thought makes me giddy. Perhaps I've always wanted to be the one everyone looks up to, instead of being in his shadow. But that idea makes me sicker and I cross myself with a quick prayer to St Jude to help Sam, who seems to me to be something of a hopeless cause.

There's a little impish face at the window. Her hair tied up in a bright yellow bow. She disappears and the front door opens. Lily is on the step clapping her hands at my arrival. If I didn't know better I'd say sometimes she looks at me with something like love in her eyes. I leap up the steps two at a time.

'Where are they Lil?' She throws her arms in the air in mock despair.

'I keep telling them to hurry up and that you'll be here any moment but they're still not ready. I've been ready for hours.' And she turns and flounces into the house, all frills and bows.

'Daddy is at the bottom of the garden and Mummy's talking to him.'

I take a breath, readying myself to get out there and drag Sam, if need be, kicking and screaming, to the ceremony. The back door slams.

'Well bloody well stay there then,' and Stella, in a rage, flies out of the kitchen, pink cheeked and wild, her hair coming undone and looking more beautiful for her fury. She barely looks at me.

'Come on. We're going,' and she sweeps Lily out of the house and into the car in what seems to be one movement.

'Leave him Wilf, he can stew in his own juices. I've had enough.' And because I hesitate for more than a second, 'I said leave him.' I run down the hall and out into their garden.

'Sam, they're only love letters mate, nothing to worry about.' I wave the leather packet but he has already gone leaving the back gate still swinging on its hinges.

I get into the car. Lily is humming a little hum in the back seat, her hands under her legs, seemingly unconcerned. I lean across Stella and put the packet into the compartment meant for gloves. She doesn't seem to notice. I can feel her boiling over next to me and I find her so hot that if I don't concentrate on driving I'm going to want to climb over into the passenger seat and take her right there in broad daylight.

I drive slowly to the recreation ground where there are stands, a stage and more bunting and banners than I've ever seen. People throng the sides of the road and as we pass they slap Ophelia's side and tip their hats at us. Stella keeps staring straight ahead and I begin to wonder whether people are whispering, seeing us arrive together, as a couple, as a family, without Sam. Stella pretends she doesn't care about the whispers but it must be killing Sam and I think she cares more than she lets on. Lily is waving at everyone and looking for all the world like a princess being bourn slowly along in her carriage, waving her little gloved hand at her people and I am glad I could bring them here in style.

We have reserved seats at the front, right next to the stage. Each seat has a card plaque with our names written in copperplate script. Even Lily has a seat and she takes it, her feet dangling, a smug smile on her little face. Sam's seat is first in the row, then Stella's and Lily's, then me and then the 1912 crew and their families. I try not to look at the seats next to Ted and Stan's wives and children. Empty, except for a single wreath on each. Everyone looks washed and scrubbed and there's nervous banter between the lads. They shift in their seats and stamp their feet, sometimes getting up and moving around, rubbing and blowing on their hands. Now and again they look at Sam's empty place but Stella says nothing. I cover for him as best I can while Lily twitters to everyone distracting us.

On the stage there is a table draped in a red cloth and filled with shining silver tankards. The vessels glow in the dull light. On the other side of the stage are some very fine seats which we suppose must be for the King. The thought of sitting so close to royalty is making me weak at the knees but unless Sam turns up I am in charge so I swagger as best I can along the line of men, quietly chivvying them and hoping to make them feel at ease, conscious I can't copy Sam's wild banter.

Samuel Tempest
2nd November 1919
Sussex Coast

The house looks as if there has been a whirlwind. It's not as if we own much but whatever we do own seems to be scattered across the floor, Lily's doll, clothes pegs, Stella's underskirts spread out in the flurry of getting ready for the big day. I try to drink it in, each nook, each piece of furniture, the fireplace with its cream and green tiles, the wall press with the wonky catch that I have been meaning to mend. The old sofa we placed in the dining room so that I can talk to Stella while she cooks, one of her flowered shawls thrown across it to cover the holes where the stuffing is coming out. I keep thinking I must be crazy. Would I want to give this all up? It's not much but it's ours. Sometimes all this makes me feel safe, unsinkable. Stella's a good woman but, I keep feeling, perhaps not my good woman. And Lily. I can't think of Lily, the way her nose crinkles when she laughs, her dimples. I close my eyes and see if I can picture them, if I can picture the house. If I can see them it will be alright. I put on my great coat and walk out of the front door. Marine Road is deserted. In the distance the band strikes up. I turn my collar up against the cold.

The people have poured themselves into every seat and standing place available. Some are even sitting on the roof of the cricket pavilion to get a bird's eye view. I scramble up the side of a grassy lump overlooking the recreation ground, trying not to be seen. I can just make out the crew, Jacky fiddling with his tie, running his fingers around the rim of his collar, unused to its tight starchiness. And there is Stella, the back of her head tilted, listening to the address by the Mayor. She sits next to my empty seat, no-one has filled it, yet. Lily is between Stella and Wilf. She bobs up and down with excitement and then leans over to Wilf to whisper in his ear. I see him bend towards her then put his finger to his mouth to shush her. He runs his hand through her hair and lays his arm around her shoulder and she snuggles in closer. The strange thing is I don't feel anything much, just a huge sense of relief that this is going on without me, that it can go on without me.

The names are being called as I turn to leave. No-one has noticed me. When my name is called Wilf pushes Lily forward on my behalf to accept the silver vessel.

The road is deserted. In the distance I can hear polite clapping and in between a raucous cheer goes up. I count each award in my head, Wilf, Ted, Jacky, Stormy, Stan, Jerry. I count each one, even the empty seats where Ted and Stan should be. I can see their faces blushing, beaming. For Stormy it will be as if he has won a football trophy. He will hold the vessel in the air and the crowds will go wild. In my head they do anyway. I don't think about Stella or Lily or Wilf.

Ophelia shines dully in the late afternoon light, the sun flashes suddenly and the metal glints like the silver vessels for a moment and then the sun is lost again behind a bank of cloud. It grows darker as if a veil has been drawn over the sky. I look around but of course there is no-one to be seen. I take the crank handle and slot it in place. I have done this so many times it's second nature but I don't have Wilf's knack with her and I wonder if she is refusing to start deliberately. After a third attempt and half wrenching my arm off she stirs with a shudder. I throw the handle in the back and leap into the front seat. Sweat gathers on my brow under the rim of my hat despite the cold. I wipe it away and feel my heart start to thunder in my chest. I've watched Wilf drive but have never had a go myself. If he can do it I can, it can't be that difficult. Come on man you can do it. Focus. But I find it hard to believe and somewhere inside there's a niggling voice saying, 'you know he's better than you, you know you can only do things when he's there to back you up.' I open a small hatch in the dashboard, the catch is fiddly and stiff. I don't expect there to be anything inside but there lies a smooth leather packet. A smooth leather packet, perhaps full of secrets. And my stomach jolts and I'm back in the shell crater with the bloody German soldier and he has a packet he is trying to give me.

I throw the car into gear, depress the clutch and we lurch down the road. When the hell did Wilf find the packet, and how long has he had it? I'm torn between feeling glad that it's here and not in the hands of some authorities but sick that Wilf had it all the time and has made me sweat. The car sputters, if I was a religious man I'd be praying she doesn't backfire. If she does it will all flood back and I'll be sunk. I concentrate on the here and now, it's only a car. I can do this. Forget about the packet; forget that he knew all along, that he had the packet all the time. Sweat runs down the side of my face but the band has struck up 'God Save the King.' Everyone is belting it out; there's no chance of anyone hearing.

The Family
2nd November 1919
Sussex Coast

'You were fantastic Lily. You didn't stumble or anything. Straight up there in front of all those people.' Stella squeezes Lily to her. The child carries the vessel as if it is something precious, like an egg that may hatch out at any moment. She holds it tenderly and a little in front of her. She gazes at the curly script in French, Dutch and English:

In honour of Samuel Tempest
Coxswain of the Lady Lucille Maythorpe
Who rescued those aboard Koning William III
18th August 1912
We thank you.

She runs her finger over the letters and flicks away a speck of dirt.

It takes them time to get to the place where they left the car, on a side street next to the recreation ground, because people keeping stopping them to look at the two vessels, Sam's and Wilf's, and to congratulate them. They slap Wilf on the back and comment about the fine speech he gave which makes him blush and look to the ground in embarrassment. Stella smiles at his quiet delight. No-one asks where Sam is. It seems that today people are sparing their blushes. No doubt behind closed doors the tongues will wag but here at least they are silent.

'Stella, you are both coming to the crew house for a drink aren't you?' She looks at Lily.

'It's alright Lily can come. I wouldn't dream of celebrating without Lily,' and he reaches out for her hand.

'I need to get back to Sam.' She smoothes her glove over the back of her hand. 'Goodness only knows what he's been doing.'

Wilf takes her elbow. 'Come on,' and steers her towards where they left the car. 'I'll come with you and then, if we can, we'll drag him to the crew house as well.'

'Wilf, where did we leave Ophelia?'

Lily runs ahead and stops at the place where the car should be. She turns towards them and shrugs, lifting her arms into the air. Wilf starts to run as if running to the empty spot will miraculously bring her back.

'Here, she was here.' Lily jumps up and down on the spot. Wilf looks about helplessly but there are no other cars on the street, hardly anyone owns a car, everyone knows this car was his Ophelia and now she is gone. Stella takes his hand and then folds herself around him, pulls him to her while he shakes with rage and loss.

They walk back to the house. Lily looking under every stone and round every corner and calling, 'Ophelia, Ophelia where are you, stop hiding.' It is all Wilf can do not to join in. Every time they pass a new turning in the

122

road he looks along it hopefully wondering if perhaps that was really where they had left her all along.

There is no-one at home. Stella walks into the garden and briefly into every room but Sam is nowhere to be seen. In temper and frustration she slams out of the house again saying, 'Come on. I think we all need a drink' and they walk hand in hand, somewhat stunned that two of the most precious things to them, Sam and Ophelia have disappeared. Lily squeezes between them and takes both of their hands, she swings on their arms and they instinctively lift her in a high spring into the air.

Samuel Tempest
2nd November 1919
Sussex Coast

Ophelia bumps her way along Marine Road, down the High Street and out of the town. As the houses melt away I feel calmer, I shrug them off like a snake shedding its skin. We follow the river, the water's edge already crispy with ice between the reeds. Then we join the coast road and climb. The grass at the sides of the road becomes springy and a few feet to starboard the cliff falls sharply away. The plan is to follow the coast road as far as I can and see where it takes me. It's a pretty fair swap, a car for a wife and child, for a whole family, a lifeboat crew even. I haven't felt this alive in years; the weight of responsibility for them dissolves. There's no doubt he'll look after them, no doubt. No more callouts, no more panic every time I hear the maroons, every time the mist crawls, wounded and gasping, up the river. Perhaps even no more fear.

As we climb higher Ophelia slows almost to a walking pace and I can't seem to organise the gears to get her to go faster. The mist that hangs around the top of the cliffs draws closer, my face is damp with it. I rub the windscreen but the water clings to it so I give up and push the glass up out of the way. It takes so much concentration up here. The wheel bumps over the verge and I veer back into the road but with the twists and turns the road keeps disappearing. It is so rutted and the car is so jumpy that I am struggling to know whether I am on the road or not. There's something about the damp air, the mist, somewhere below a fog horn blares out but even this is muffled and suffocated and I can't tell if it's below me or above me, everything is disorientated in the fog and I don't know if it's a fog horn or an enemy blast. I'm back on The *Lucy May* crashing along in the chop, the engine sputtering. I stand up to stare out to sea to gain a clue from the position of sea and sky, forgetting the controls, forgetting Wilf is not on the engine, forgetting that Jacky is not at the helm, forgetting, forgetting. Something in the boat explodes and I leap.

Wilf and Stella stumble from the lifeboat hut elated and singing. Wilf carries Lily wrapped in a blanket, she is completely oblivious to the noise. They shush each other playfully.

'Wilf.'

He turns and Jacky waves wildly at him.

'Jacky mate, it's late,' and then he hears it as if in a dream, the sound like blades on ice, the skater shooting away. Then the silence. She knows too before the maroon is up and she has taken the warm and sleeping bundle from him. The explosion is extra loud because they are so close. The gulls rise up, white and whirling flakes in the night sky. He turns to run.

'It's a car,' Jacky shouts catching the sou'wester thrown at him. He throws one at Wilf, 'it's gone over the cliff.'

19th December 1919
Sussex Coast

They have stopped crying now. Relief mixed up with loss. They have dealt with it differently. Stella defiantly rearranging furniture, planning the re-launch of her dive show in the spring, while still bearing the tearing hole in her chest. Wilf disappeared too for a few days throwing Stella and Lily into turmoil. He spent them walking, wracked with guilt, praying and drinking. He returned one evening, red-eyed and exhausted. Stella's anger thawed and she held him through his pain.

Ophelia was recovered battered and scarred from her plummet over the cliff edge but Wilf cannot look at her. She sits in the lean-to waiting for him to see if he can bare to restore her. There was no survivors and no sign that Sam had been there but they both knew he had.

It is nearly Christmas and Stella is attempting to make a plum pudding.

'It will be dreadful, you know it will. Are you sure you want me to make it?' But she shoos them out of the house anyway to forage for ivy and laurel and fir to use as decorations. They walk hand in hand, Lily skipping and hoping for snow. Wilf tries not to fuel her dreams by saying they have never had snow this close to the sea. She stops and her eyes fill with tears. Stella had been filling her head full of nonsense about snow and reindeer and sleighs.

'Would you like to see Ophelia?' Wilf wonders if a battered car can take away the pain of no snow but her face beams and they drag their foliage up to the lean-to. She scampers up to the car whispering, 'Ophelia, Ophelia,' and strokes the bruised metalwork. Wilf lifts her into the passenger seat, the leather is hard and dry and cracked. Lily reaches for the compartment meant for keeping driving gloves. It won't open of course, the dashboard is caved in and she looks up at Wilf expecting him to make it work.

'There's nothing inside, I don't own driving gloves.' But he gives a tug anyway and the door itself comes away. Lily goes to reach inside but he remembers the packet and pushes his hand in first. The packet has gone but a gold band falls into the palm of his hand.

Lily looks up at him, 'Uncle Wilf, isn't that Daddy's wedding ring?' and he closes his fist tight around the band. The wind gusts in from the sea and the clouds hold a promise of snow. Wilf swings Lily out of the car. He takes her hand for the walk home and, for safe keeping, slips the ring onto his finger.